"You okay over there?
voice slipped throug

"I'm tired but I'll be ok." B
her house, her stomach ten
parked in the driveway—so   ...king home
and talking to her dad first.

"Looks like company," Patrick said, trying to sound
cheery.

Gracie wished she could smile. "Looks like a lynching
to me."

She reached for the truck door, but hesitated. One last
minute to catch her breath…or maybe one last chance
to keep running.

"I'm with you, Gracie." Patrick's voice immediately
stilled the knots in her stomach. It was odd, knowing
that this man—her boss, practically a stranger—would
be at her side, made Gracie feel more secure than she'd
ever felt with her ex-fiancé.

Then, Patrick stepped out of the truck, and Gracie
guessed she had to go, too. Time to stop running.

**The Heart of Main Street: They're rebuilding
the town one step—and heart—at a time.**

Books by Brenda Minton

Love Inspired

Trusting Him
His Little Cowgirl
A Cowboy's Heart
The Cowboy Next Door
Rekindled Hearts
Blessings of the Season
  "The Christmas Letter"
Jenna's Cowboy Hero
The Cowboy's Courtship
The Cowboy's Sweetheart
Thanksgiving Groom
The Cowboy's Family

The Cowboy's Homecoming
Christmas Gifts
  *"Her Christmas Cowboy"
*The Cowboy's Holiday
  Blessing
*The Bull Rider's Baby
*The Rancher's Secret Wife
*The Cowboy's Healing Ways
*The Cowboy Lawman
The Boss's Bride

*Cooper Creek

BRENDA MINTON

started creating stories to entertain herself during hour-long rides on the school bus. In high school she wrote romance novels to entertain her friends. The dream grew and so did her aspirations to become an author. She started with notebooks, handwritten manuscripts and characters that refused to go away until their stories were told. Eventually she put away the pen and paper and got down to business with the computer. The journey took a few years, with some encouragement and rejection along the way—as well as a lot of stubbornness on her part. In 2006 her dream to write for Love Inspired Books came true. Brenda lives in the rural Ozarks with her husband, three kids and an abundance of cats and dogs. She enjoys a chaotic life that she wouldn't trade for anything—except, on occasion, a beach house in Texas. You can stop by and visit at her website, www.brendaminton.net.

The Boss's Bride
Brenda Minton

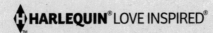

Special thanks and acknowlegment to Brenda Minton for her contribution to The Heart of Main Street series.

Recycling programs
for this product may
not exist in your area.

™ LOVE INSPIRED BOOKS

ISBN-13: 978-0-373-81714-6

THE BOSS'S BRIDE

www.LoveInspiredBooks.com

Printed in U.S.A.

Delight thyself also in the Lord, and he shall give thee the desires of thine heart.
—*Psalms* 37:4

In memory of my sweet friend Alice.

Friendships can be found in the most amazing ways at the most amazing times. I encourage you all to take time for older citizens confined to long-term care facilities. You'll be blessed.

Prologue

~⚭~

Gracie Wilson stood in the center of a Sunday school classroom at the Bygones Community Church. Her friend Janie Lawson adjusted her veil and again wiped at tears.

"You look beautiful."

"Do I?" Gracie glanced in the full-length mirror that hung on the door of the supply cabinet and suppressed a shudder. The dress was hideous and she hadn't picked it.

"Of course you do. You look like a fairy princess."

Gracie groaned. "Is this another height joke?"

Janie hugged her tight for one second. "Not at all. You look beautiful. And you look miserable. It's your wedding day. You should be smiling."

Gracie smiled, but she knew it was a poor attempt at best. The frown on Janie's face confirmed it. She exhaled and looked again at her reflection in the mirror. Janie was right; a bride shouldn't look sad.

"Gracie, what's wrong?" Janie walked up behind her and peeked over her shoulder so that their reflections stared back at them.

"Nothing. I'm good." She leaned her cheek against Janie's hand on her shoulder. "Other than the fact that you've moved one hundred miles away and I never get to see you."

What else could she say? Everyone in Bygones, Kansas, and probably for miles around, thought she'd landed the catch of the century. Trent Morgan was handsome, charming and came from money. She should be thrilled to be marrying him. Six months ago she had been thrilled. Five months ago she'd still been happy.

But then she'd started to notice little signs. She should have put the wedding on hold the moment she noticed those signs. She should have slowed down and not worried so much about what everyone else would think. And when she knew for certain, she should have put a stop to the entire thing. But she hadn't. Because once the wedding wheels had been put in motion, she hadn't known how to stop it all from happening.

It made her feel weak. And she'd never been a weak person.

"You're not convincing me." Janie smiled tenderly, a best-friend smile reflected from the mirror. Gracie turned to face her friend, the skirt of the dress pushing them apart.

"I'm just tired, Janie. I mean, it's been a long three months of wedding planning, right?" Did she sound convincing?

"And Mrs. Morgan isn't a dream of a woman to deal with." Janie gave an exaggerated shudder to prove her point.

"Exactly." Gracie twirled in the lace creation that had a skirt that made her look like a dinner bell or a Southern belle—she wasn't sure which. "Do you care if I have a few minutes alone?"

"Of course not," Janie gave her another hug. "But not too long. You dad is outside, and when I came in to check on you, the seats were filling up out there."

"I won't be long. I just need a minute to catch my breath."

"Of course you do. And just think, after today you'll be going to Hawaii and you'll have a week on the beach to catch your breath. And then you'll move to Manhattan and your new home."

Gracie smiled and nodded her head, trying to pretend the idea excited her. A week in Hawaii. On the beach. With Trent.

Janie smiled back at her and then the door

to the classroom closed. And for the first time in days, Gracie was alone. She looked around the room with the bright yellow walls and posters from the Sunday school curriculum. She stopped at the poster of David and Goliath. Her favorite. She'd love to have that kind of faith, the kind that knocked down giants.

She knew a few Davids. Ann Mars was a faith giant. And Miss Coraline Connolly. They both believed the town of Bygones could be saved. Not with stones and a slingshot but with new businesses and new people.

And of course those new businesses made her think of her boss at The Fixer-Upper. Patrick Fogerty, one of the most genuinely nice people she'd ever met.

She closed her eyes and took a deep breath. Today was her wedding day. Instead of worrying, she had to remember back to when she met Trent and how love had felt then. Not how it felt now—sadly lacking because he'd not only pulled away, he'd betrayed her trust. A knock on the door interrupted her thoughts.

"You almost ready, Gracie?" her dad called through the door.

"Almost."

She opened the window, just to let in fresh air. She leaned out, breathing the hint of autumn, enjoying the breeze on her face. She looked across the grassy lawn and saw…

FREEDOM.

She shook her head at the word. That was the wrong word. A bride shouldn't be thinking of freedom. She should be thinking of happy-ever-after with the man she loved. The word ached deep inside, mocking her. *Love.* It meant something, to love someone, to want to be with them forever. It meant loyalty.

She closed her eyes and thought back to that day one month ago when she'd meant to surprise Trent. She'd packed a lunch for them. She'd thought a picnic would be romantic. Instead she sat in her car watching him and then she'd eased out of the parking space, driving away as if she hadn't seen anything. That moment had confirmed her suspicions.

It all added up. He had been seeing someone else while she'd been busy at home, planning their wedding. He had texted the other woman while they'd been sampling cakes at the Sweet Dreams Bakery. He'd called her while he and Gracie had dinner with his parents.

Gracie hadn't known how to end a relationship just weeks short of the wedding.

But now she did.

Quiet as a mouse, she slid herself and the

hoopskirt through the window. Once she stood on the grass outside the window, her heart began to pound. She thought about how wrong this was. She thought about all the money Mrs. Morgan had spent.

She thought of how things would have been different if her own mother had been alive and she'd had a woman to turn to, to talk to. If she didn't feel so responsible for everyone else.

It hadn't been her plan to sneak around the side of the church, to look out at the crowded parking lot. The limo was already decorated with cans, streamers and painted windows; two teenage boys were finishing up with cans of shaving cream. She hadn't planned to slip away and then run as fast as she could down a side street.

But she did run.

And she felt freer than she had in months. She felt the breeze on her face, the coolness of the air, and knew she couldn't marry Trent Morgan. But she didn't know where to go or what to do now that she'd left her groom standing in the sanctuary of the church waiting for a bride who wouldn't be walking down the aisle. She only knew that she couldn't go through with this wedding.

Chapter One

The stockroom of The Fixer-Upper hardware store was dark, warm and strangely peaceful. Gracie sat on a stool, staring down at the white dress that hadn't made it down the aisle. She shifted the skirt, all lace and silk, the type of creation she never would have picked on her own. The only things of her own choosing were her white cowboy boots with sequins and the crystal ribbon on the flowers.

She studied the bouquet Trent's mother had picked, so different from the daisies Gracie had wanted. When Gracie had sneaked into The Fixer-Upper, she'd tossed the bouquet on a worktable. Even from several feet away, she could smell the sweetness of the flowers, a reminder that this had never really been her wedding. Even the yellow roses, which would have been okay, had been enhanced with a few exotic blooms. Mrs. Morgan had a thing for over-the-top.

From the church to the decorations, Trent's mother had made all the decisions. Mrs. Morgan, wife of a prominent surgeon, had taken charge. After all, as Mrs. Morgan liked to point out, Gracie didn't have a mother of her own to take care of these things. And because Gracie's father's granary was struggling, like every other business in Bygones, Kansas, the Morgan family had been footing the bill for their only son to marry Gracie Wilson.

Gracie smiled as she leaned back against the wall and closed her eyes. She'd finally made a decision of her own. She'd made the decision to bail on the whole dreadful affair.

It seemed as if everyone was counting on this marriage. It had definitely been a big help to the Bygones economy, thanks to the Morgans. *My dad.* Thinking of him, she felt guilty. He'd been happy, thinking she would never have to work hard again. She was marrying up, he'd said. She'd be set for life, her brother Evan had added.

She'd never agreed with her dad about marrying up. Her dad and her five brothers were the cream of the crop. Very few men could compete with those men of hers. Trent Morgan might have money but he was far from marrying "up" for Gracie. He'd proven more than once that he wasn't the man she wanted to share her dreams or her life with.

She drew in a deep breath and she didn't cry. As difficult as tomorrow would be for her, for her family, today she could breathe. She had made the right decision. She'd made the decision she'd been afraid to make weeks ago when she first caught him cheating. She'd made the decision she should have made months ago when first she realized something was wrong.

She'd started the relationship with Trent thinking it would be perfect. But they'd been two different people. She knew how to rely on her faith. He used his faith as a disguise.

She had tried to do the right thing for everyone. But she hadn't done the right thing for herself.

She only hoped she still had a job here at The Fixer-Upper hardware store. She hoped her boss, Patrick Fogerty, hadn't replaced her. She would definitely need the money, because she had a feeling Mrs. Morgan would want to be reimbursed for the wedding that hadn't happened.

Her dad couldn't afford the expense.

Somehow she'd make this right. She would get her life back. Tomorrow she'd admit to Miss

Coraline Connolly, retired principal of the Bygones school system, that she'd been right. She and Ann Mars, owner of the This 'N' That, had both questioned her in the past few days, telling her she didn't look as happy as a bride-to-be ought to.

Outside The Fixer-Upper she could hear cars. People were probably looking for her. She guessed her dad would have gone home to search in all of her old hiding places. No one would think to check for her in the hardware store, a business that had been in town for only two months, with an owner few people really knew.

They'd like him once they got to know him, she thought, once they realized he wasn't just a city person looking for a fresh start. He was a decent man who really wanted to be a part of a community. She thought that about all the new business owners in Bygones. From the coffee shop to the bakery, they had made the town better. They were giving her hometown hope. The folks in Bygones needed hope.

She needed hope. She closed her eyes and prayed, something she should have been doing more of. She should have paid attention to her nagging doubts about this marriage. She should have listened to God. Instead she'd listened to everyone else, to all the people telling her how great it would be to marry a man like Trent.

Gracie swiped a hand across her eyes. A tear or two slipped down her cheeks, not for the marriage that wouldn't be, but for her dad, her family and her community. She thought about her mom and how things would have been different if Eva Wilson had lived.

The door chime dinged on the wall across from her. Someone had opened the front door of the hardware store. She scooted to the edge of the stool and glanced at the back door, her only way to escape. But running out the back door would set off an alarm, and the overworked, understaffed local police didn't need more drama. They were probably busy looking for her.

She reached for a three-foot length of rebar and held it tight in her hand, just in case the person coming in thought they could rip the place off, since everyone in town was otherwise occupied. There had been some vandalism lately. As quiet as Bygones used to be, a break-in wouldn't be so surprising in this economy. The door to the storeroom opened. She held the rebar close, took a deep breath and waited.

Patrick Fogerty stepped into the room, all six feet four inches of him. He looked around and then spotted her. Gracie shrugged as she watched her boss take a few steps into the room, his ruggedly handsome face masked in shadows, his dark hair a little messy from the wind.

For the first time she really wanted to cry. It was a strange mixture of relief, sadness, guilt and anger that wrapped itself up inside of her like tangled string, none of it really making any sense. Tears sprang to her eyes and she blinked them away. Patrick offered her a sympathetic smile and that was when the tears really began to flow.

Gracie Wilson stared up at Patrick, her wide, dark eyes filling with tears. He watched her for a long minute, surprised to see her sitting in the stockroom of his store. When she hadn't walked down the aisle, everyone had been surprised. Everyone, that is, except Ann Mars. He'd been sitting next to her in the church, and for whatever reason, she hadn't seemed all that shocked. She'd told him that it was because she was in her eighties and she knew a thing or two about life.

Miss Mars, instead of being worried, had seemed relieved. He'd thought he heard a few sighs of relief throughout the sanctuary of Bygones Community Church.

"Are you going to hit me with that rebar?" he asked, because he didn't know what else to say. Damsels in distress were not typically his cup of tea.

What else could he say to the woman he'd known for only a couple of months? She'd been recommended by Ann Mars, his worthy representative and guide to all things Bygones. Ann had promised him an employee who would be on time, work hard and know how to fix anything as well as bring in customers. She'd picked the right person.

Gracie Wilson could handle tools, she could handle customers, and she even seemed to know how to handle him. She'd kept him from giving up on this venture. After all, he was a city boy, born and raised. Moving to Bygones, starting a new business in a town that was struggling financially, that took faith. When his seemed to be in short supply, she loaned him hers the way neighbors loaned a cup of sugar in Bygones, Kansas.

He'd made a commitment. A business of his own in trade for a commitment to stay for two years and make it work. There were several new businesses in Bygones. They were painted, remodeled and hopefully a cure for a town that didn't want to lose everything.

"I was prepared for a burglar," she whispered as tears trickled down her cheeks.

He stood there for a long minute, unsure of what to do next. Call the police? Call Ann Mars, his Save Our Streets sponsor?

She shifted on the stool. "Say something."

"Gracie," he cleared his throat, "I guess I'm surprised to see you here."

She looked up, smiling a little as she brushed tears from her cheeks. She looked tinier than ever in the white creation of a dress, her dark hair pulled back with rhinestone clips and strings of pearls.

"I think there are probably a lot of people surprised," she said, brushing away her tears.

"Yes, surprised and worried. They're searching for you." He focused on the rebar she still had a death grip on. "Other than the ones who decided to take advantage of the reception."

"It should be a good party."

"What happened?"

"I couldn't marry him." She laughed and then sobbed. "I'm going to be in big trouble."

"Seems to me the trouble would have been marrying him if you had doubts."

She nodded but didn't speak. The tears were streaming down her cheeks again, and he wondered if her doubts were real or if she just had cold feet and needed a few minutes to get her thoughts together.

"Can I help?"

She shook her head. "No. I mean, there's really nothing anyone can do. I just can't marry him."

"Are you sure?" He cleared his throat, not at all sure what else to say in a situation such as this. He'd never had little sisters. He'd dated but never been married.

He'd learned one thing about women: sometimes they walked when things looked difficult. At least, that was what had happened to him.

He didn't think Gracie was the type to skip out on someone just because it got a little difficult.

Sitting on the stool, she looked smaller than her barely five feet, especially in the billowy white dress that didn't seem to suit her style. Not that he was a guy who paid much attention to style. But even he could recognize when a woman needed someone, though.

He pushed aside misgivings and reached to hug her. First he took the rebar from her hand and set it on the worktable. She leaned into his shoulder and he wrapped his arms around her, keeping his face out of the protruding objects that decorated her hair. Avoiding the light scent of her fragrance took more effort. It matched the softness of her skin and the sweet way she leaned against him.

For a guy who didn't notice much, unless it had to do with home remodeling or electrical problems, he noticed a lot in those few minutes holding Gracie.

"I can't marry him," she finally whispered against his shoulder and then she backed out of his embrace. "But I'm going to have to face this."

"Yes, I guess you will." He reached for a roll of paper towels on the shelf and pulled off a few sheets for her to wipe her eyes. "I don't have a handkerchief."

She smiled through her tears and then laughed. "Wouldn't that be chivalrous if you did? Maybe a little too cliché?"

"I guess that's a good reason to never offer a woman a handkerchief. What guy wants to be cliché?"

"You could never be cliché." She smiled as she said it, dabbing her eyes with paper towels that were less than soft. "My dad is going to be embarrassed. Mrs. Morgan will be furious. I wonder if there's a bus out of this town tonight."

"I don't think a bus comes anywhere near Bygones. And if you caught a bus, who would work for me?"

"You haven't replaced me?"

"Of course not. And if you're up to it, I'll need you here Monday morning. Remember, you had that great idea to have the block party in a few weeks. I can't do that without you."

"You could."

"Yeah, but people trust you. They aren't always trusting of the city guy who has moved in and wants their business."

"They'll learn that you can be trusted."

"Thanks, Gracie." He reached for her hand and helped her down from the stool. "I like the boots."

"Thank you. I picked them out." She twirled in the dress that looked like white lace gone crazy. "I did not pick this. I think it makes me look like a bad version of Cinderella at the ball."

"It isn't that bad."

She wrinkled her nose at him. "It is that bad. You're just being nice."

"Okay, I'm being nice. I am a nice guy. Haven't you heard?"

She smiled up at him. She was more than a foot shorter than him, with a pixie face and dark eyes that could tease or flash with humor. Sometimes those eyes flashed fire if something got her riled up. She was twenty-four, ten years younger than his thirty-four years. She sometimes seemed younger, but more often seemed a decade older.

He knew she'd gone through a lot. She'd lost her mom fourteen years ago. Miss Coraline had given him tidbits and told him to take care of her girl, because Gracie acted strong but she needed to be able to let other people be strong for her. He'd gotten a lot of advice from Coraline Connolly since he'd moved to Bygones.

"You are a nice guy, Patrick." Gracie sighed and reached back for the veil that hung from a hook on the wall. "And my name is going to be mud. I'm glad I have one friend left."

"Want me to drive you home?"

She nodded. "Please. Unless of course you're willing to help me run away from Bygones. Far away."

"Sorry, I'm here for at least two years and I'd like for you to be here, too. If you stay, you know I'll have your back. I'll be here for you."

"Thank you. And I'm going to help you find a wife. You need a wife. A good country woman that can cook biscuits and gravy."

"The person who just ran from her own wedding wants to arrange one for me?"

"I guess you have a point. I don't think I'm the poster child for encouraging someone to take the walk down the aisle."

He grinned at that. "No, probably not."

"Can you get me out of here without everyone seeing me?"

"In that dress?"

She looked down. "I guess not."

"I have sweatpants and a T-shirt you could change into. They'll be a little big, but not as obvious."

"And then I can leave the dress here. Mrs. Morgan will want to return it if she can."

"Or maybe you'll change your mind?"

"About the dress or Trent? I don't think I'll be taking either of them down the aisle."

He didn't know what to say to that. He'd known her all of two months and he didn't think he should be the one standing here having this conversation. There were people in town who had known her all her life. The same people who had shared stories with him of a rough-and-rowdy little girl turned woman. A woman who seemed to know her mind and be able to handle almost any situation.

Sometimes when Patrick looked at her, he saw seven shades of vulnerable in her dark eyes and a whole lot of sadness. He thought maybe the only other person who saw that look was Miss Coraline. The retired principal seemed to see a lot in everyone. He guessed it probably had made her very good at her job.

He shook himself from those thoughts and gave Gracie an easy smile. "I'll get the clothes and you can change in the restroom."

"Thank you, Patrick." She had that soft look in her eyes, the one that said she might cry again if he said the wrong thing or got too close.

He backed away, made sorry excuses and headed for the exit.

He'd come to Bygones because his family business had closed down after a big-box store full of discount lumber and building supplies moved into their suburban Detroit neighborhood, the neighborhood that had supported them for years.

Bygones was his future, his dream. It seemed literally the answer to his prayers: a small-town hardware store, close neighbors, a place to start over.

He hadn't realized moving to a small town meant getting tangled up in the lives of the people who lived there. He hadn't realized they would pull him in and make him such a part of their families and community.

More than anything, he hadn't planned on someone like Gracie Wilson storming into his life.

Chapter Two

Gracie sat in the passenger seat of Patrick's Ford truck. Her dress was hanging at the store, covered in plastic. She had donned gigantic-size sweatpants and a T-shirt that hung to her knees. She'd used a stapler to narrow the waist of the pants and she'd tied a knot in the tail of the shirt to shorten it.

As they drove through the now darkened streets of Bygones, it was hard for her to recognize this as the town she'd grown up in. The brick of the stores downtown, one whole section of buildings, had been painted a creamy color. Awnings of various colors brightened the exteriors. There was a coffee shop—who would have thought they'd have one of those in a small farming community?—a bakery, a flower shop, a bookstore and a pet shop. In Bygones? There were days that she drove to work, parked her truck and wondered if she was in the wrong town.

The streets had been repaired, there were new streetlights, and the park had been cleaned and spruced up. It was window dressing, just like the marriage she'd almost had. Could pretty stores and some remodeling actually save a town that was dying? Young people were moving to cities to find jobs, people were losing farms and houses, tax revenue was down, and the school and police station were in danger of closing.

The biggest hit to the town had been the closing of Randall Manufacturing. A lot of her friends had moved when the factory closed.

"Do you really not know who did this, Patrick?"

He glanced her way, looking pretty confused. "The wedding?"

"No, the town, the businesses. Who put up the money for Save Our Streets?"

"Not a clue."

She didn't continue the conversation. She was too tired for the words. Someone, no one knew who but everyone speculated, had started this renovation project, bringing in new businesses and new people. Someone thought they could save Bygones. And as happy as some people were, others weren't so happy with change and an influx of new citizens.

She closed her eyes and let the town and the gloomy thoughts slip behind her.

"You okay over there?" Patrick's strong, husky voice slipped through the cab of the truck and she nodded.

"I'm good. I'm tired but I'm good." She opened her eyes and looked at the strong profile of her boss. He glanced her way briefly.

Friends had teased her about working for the hottest hardware-store owner in the state, as they liked to call him. They all found random reasons to come into the store. The women in the town were going to keep The Fixer-Upper in business the way the young people would keep the coffee shop going.

"I could use you full-time at the store." His attention was back on the road.

"I could use full-time. I'm going to have to pay back the Morgans, and my dad could really use my help."

"That's a lot to take on, Gracie."

"I know." She tried to think of a time in her life when she wasn't thinking about how to fix things.

She'd learned early how to cook, how to do laundry, repair jeans and shirts for her brothers, and keep them from fighting. She'd learned how to make her dad smile. Jacob Wilson was a good man. He'd done his best after Gracie's mom passed away. They'd all done their best.

She sighed and closed her eyes again.

"If I could I'd give you a raise. Maybe soon."

"Thank you." She looked out the window at passing farmland. There were fields of sunflowers ready for harvest, soybeans, corn and wheat. Her dad ran the granary that took in the seed and the grain, holding it in storage for farmers and selling the surplus.

Business had been bad. A few farmers had lost their land to foreclosure, meaning the loss of business for her dad. And the summer had been dry, burning up some crops before they could be harvested. Irrigation had saved the larger farms.

"You know, I'm not sure where you live."

She looked his way again. "Sorry. It's a half mile farther. There's a mailbox that looks like a barn. It's on the right."

"Gotcha."

She wasn't looking forward to going home. The closer they got, the more her stomach tightened into knots. Patrick flipped on his turn signal and headed up the half-mile-long driveway to the farmhouse that had been in her family for over a hundred years. The place looked lonely, sitting in the middle of fields of corn. There were two big trees in the yard and behind the house were a silo and a few outbuildings, plus the old barn that she used to love to play in.

She took in a deep breath as she looked at the house, lights burning in various windows. A half-dozen cars were parked in the driveway. So much for sneaking home and talking to her dad

"This doesn't look good," she murmured as the truck stopped.

"Looks like company."

She wished she could smile, but she couldn't. "Looks like a lynching to me."

"I can go in with you."

She smiled because he already had the keys out of the ignition. She often teased him because he was the only guy in Bygones who always removed his keys and locked his truck doors. She called him a city boy, but he wasn't really. He fit Bygones. It was as if he'd always been here.

"Okay, let's get this over with. But I won't blame you if you want to leave." She reached for the truck door, but hesitated before pushing it open. One last minute to catch her breath.

"I'm with you, Gracie." He stepped out of the truck and she guessed she had to go, too.

The only good thing about this moment, other than Patrick at her side, was that the Morgans didn't appear to be here. She couldn't exactly be relieved, but that knowledge did help her to take an easy breath as she and Patrick walked up to the two-story farmhouse.

They were almost to the porch when another car pulled up and parked. Gracie turned and groaned as the driver stepped out. Whitney Leigh, ace reporter. Or as ace as a reporter for the *Bygones Gazette* could be. And Gracie's wedding, once the biggest social event of the year, was now the biggest scandal of the decade.

The screen door of the farmhouse squeaked open. Gracie turned to face her older brother Max. He stepped onto the porch, his girlfriend, Lizzy, close on his heels.

"About time you showed yourself. Dad's still in town looking for you."

"I'll call him." Gracie glanced at her brother and then at Whitney, almost on them now, her blond hair pulled back in a tight ponytail and her glasses settled on her pretty nose.

Gracie had always liked Whitney, just not right now.

"Gracie, can we talk?" Whitney smiled at Patrick, a quick smile, not the kind most women gave him.

"I'd rather not, Whitney."

"But I have a lot of questions and people in town are going to want to know."

"Know·what, Whitney?" Max stepped closer to Gracie's side and suddenly her brothers were there. Caleb, who was Max's twin, Jason and Daniel. But not Evan. He hadn't even planned on attending her wedding.

Gracie's eyes stung with unshed tears because Evan had been right. For a year he'd told her something was off with Trent Morgan.

Patrick stepped away. She knew he intended to leave. She had family. He was just her boss.

Of course she didn't need him there with her.

Whitney moved in a little closer, her eyes darting from Wilson to Wilson, and she wasn't intimidated. "I think most people are going to ask you if you plan on going through with the wedding. Did you just have a case of cold feet?"

"I'm not going to marry Trent Morgan."

Whitney nodded and then looked at Patrick, a smile appearing on her pretty face. Gracie groaned at that look, but before she could respond, Whitney had another question.

"Is there any reason for running from your own wedding, Gracie? Have you met someone else?"

It was on Gracie's mind to tell the whole truth but she couldn't. What good would it do to drag

Trent Morgan through the mud? It would only serve one purpose—to make her feel better.

"I haven't met anyone else, Whitney. You know me better than that. And I'm not going to share the reason I left. Could we please stop this? I'm not news. This is Bygones, not Hollywood, and my wedding isn't a big deal."

"It's the lack of a wedding that makes this news, Gracie."

"Only for a week. Only until someone's house gets vandalized or someone TPs the school."

Whitney smiled sympathetically and touched her arm. "I hope for your sake that's the truth."

"Thank you. And now I have to talk to my family."

Max handed her his cell phone. "It's Dad."

She held the phone for a minute because she didn't know what she would say to her dad, other than to assure him she was okay. Patrick moved away from her.

"I'll see you Monday?" he said as he stepped down off the porch.

"Of course. And thank you."

"You're welcome."

Gracie watched Patrick walk to his truck. She would see him Monday at work. And it would be as if this wedding never happened. But then, she guessed the wedding didn't happen.

* * *

The last thing Patrick expected on Monday morning was the line of people on the sidewalk waiting to get into his store. He glanced out, watching as more cars parked on the crowded street. A few people held coffee cups from the Cozy Cup Café and more than one carried bags from the Sweet Dreams Bakery.

He hated to say it, but the Bygones Runaway Bride had done more for the Bygones economy than just about every other project the town had come up with. He wouldn't allow himself to think that it was another ploy by the good citizens, meant to bring business to the failing community.

Miss Coraline Connolly had had some crazy ideas, but that would be going too far.

Someone pounded on the back door of the building. He glanced at his watch. Still twenty minutes before he opened at nine o'clock. He gave the crowd one last look, shook his head in amazement and headed for the stockroom. He guessed Gracie had seen the crowd and had opted to enter through the back door in the alley behind the store.

When he opened the door, it was Miss Coraline, retired principal of the Bygones school system and determined optimist. He'd never met a woman so determined. And she had with her that tiny dynamo of a woman Ann Mars, owner of the This 'N' That shop. Ann, an active woman in her mid-eighties, had been assigned to be his host and helper when he moved to town.

The two women were both faithful Christians, and both loved their town, but they were as different as night and day. Miss Coraline, with her short gray hair and dress suits, always seemed in charge. Ann Mars coiled her long white hair on top of her head, smelled like sugar cookies and could sweet-talk a snake out of its skin. She was genuinely nice and made a person want to do things for her. Coraline was dignified. Ann was less than five feet tall and slightly stooped.

"Welcome, ladies. To what do I owe this pleasure?"

Miss Coraline spoke first, which seemed to be how she was wired. "As if you don't know, Patrick Fogerty. We're here to help with crowd control."

He looked at the two women and tried to remain serious. But he smiled; he couldn't help it. He was picturing the tiny Ann Mars holding back the crowd waiting outside his store. A good wind would blow her over and that crowd could trample her.

"I'm not sure why I would need crowd control. Isn't it just your average Monday in Bygones?"

Ann Mars wagged her finger at him. "Do not play with us, young man. You saw that crowd out there, and it isn't your…"

She turned a little pink and Miss Coraline cleared her throat. "What she means to say is that as handsome as you are, that crowd isn't here to buy drills or nails. They're here to see if Gracie shows up for work."

"I'm sure she'll be here." He reached for his store apron, dark green with deep pockets for tools and other items he might need.

"She's going to need you," Coraline Connolly said with a lift of her chin. He hadn't known her long but that look seemed to mean she meant business.

"I think she has plenty of people." The back door eased open and he smiled at his two friends. "And here she is."

Miss Coraline pulled the door open and Gracie stepped into the room, her face a little pink and her short dark hair a windblown halo around her face.

"Oh, Miss Coraline, Miss Mars, I didn't expect you."

Ann Mars didn't say a word; she grabbed

Gracie in a tight hug and held her until the moment became pretty uncomfortable. Patrick glanced at his watch. It was nearly time to open. He looked at the complicated group of females standing in front of him and he wondered why he had ever thought small-town life would be simpler.

"There's a crowd out front," Gracie said after she'd wiggled free from the arms of Ann Mars.

"Yes, there is, and I guess we know why they're here." Ann pursed her lips and snorted.

"To buy hardware supplies?" Gracie dropped her purse on the table where she'd left her flowers two nights ago. The flowers were now wilted, a symbol of the wedding that hadn't been. She picked them up and started to dump them in the trash but first she removed the ribbon.

A symbol of her own stubbornness. She'd had to fight for that ribbon, so she might as well keep it.

"Are you okay?" Patrick stood next to her, his words quiet in his husky voice.

"I'm good. A little nervous. But I can't hide forever."

"Gracie, you're going to have to face this." Coraline edged close and gave the flowers a disgusted look. "What a mess. But you did the right thing. I don't know why you did it, and that's your business, but I never felt good about you marrying that young man."

Gracie kissed Miss Coraline's cheek. "Thank you. I guess I didn't, either."

"So now we face the fallout. Together." Coraline linked her arm with Gracie's. "You have us. And you have Patrick. And someday you'll meet the man of your dreams and have a wonderful life."

"I think I'll take a break from romance," Gracie murmured, unable to look up for fear of seeing Patrick.

"Are you okay?" Ann slipped close. "You look flushed."

"I'm good. I just need to get back to work and get past this."

Patrick glanced at his watch. "Time to open up."

"And face the music," Coraline said with a bright smile.

"I don't think we want to talk about music," Ann Mars whispered to her friend. "It might make her think of the wedding."

Gracie smiled as she followed Patrick into the main part of the store. When she saw the crowd at the doors, she faltered. She had expected people to be curious. She hadn't expected a mob.

"This is more than I expected. From the street it looked like a few people, not a crowd."

"They've been out there for an hour." Patrick paused, looking from her to the door and back to her. Gracie wanted to sink into the floor. "You could take today off."

She shook her head. "No, I'm staying. If I don't face it today, I'll have to face it tomorrow or the next day."

Eventually she'd also have to face Trent and his parents. They'd called yesterday, but her dad had been firm, telling them they could wait a few days and then informing them that this big wedding had been their idea, not his and not Gracie's, so the expense was theirs.

Her dad hadn't asked a lot of questions about why she'd left the church the way she had. He'd never been comfortable with father-daughter talks and had counted on ladies in town to take those discussions off his hands.

She swallowed past the lump that settled in her throat as Patrick turned the dead bolt and opened the door. The crowd poured into the store, more interested in her than the great sale on power drills.

Those drills were a really great buy.

A young woman approached Gracie, elbowing people out of her way as she moved through the crowd towing two young children behind her. Gracie didn't know her but the brunette smiled as if they'd been friends forever.

"Can I help you?" Gracie cleared her throat to get the words out.

"Yes, you can. I need to know how to fix a window that lets in cold air. I need help."

A window? Gracie hadn't expected that. She breathed a sigh of relief and led the woman to the section of the store with sealants, window plastic and other do-it-yourself items.

"Here we go. Is it just one window?"

The woman looked around, glaring at customers who tried to get close enough to listen. "More than one. And I have to do this job myself. With two kids and a husband who decided he might as well be single, I'm on my own. Good for you, Gracie Wilson, for running before the wedding."

"Oh, I…" She didn't know what to say.

"It's better to walk away from a wedding than walk away from a marriage."

"I see, well, yes." Heat crawled up her cheeks. "Let's see. Do you want the plastic? It's easy to put it up. A few tacks, a hair dryer and you'll save yourself a lot of money this winter."

"I think that's perfect. Do you think I can put it up myself?"

"I put it up every winter on our old farmhouse."

"That's great." The young woman gave her a hug and then hurried away with plastic and two children.

Gracie started to turn but a woman grabbed her arm and gave her a big hug. Gracie squirmed away and saw that it was a friend she'd gone to school with.

"Gracie, I don't know what happened, but we're behind you."

Gracie opened her mouth, but she couldn't explain. It was private and it still hurt too much to think about. She wasn't a hero. She wasn't suddenly wild and crazy, breezing through life without thinking.

"Is it because your boss is such a hunk?" Lacey Clark asked. Lacey ran a day care but she'd lost half her clients when Randall Manufacturing closed.

She wondered if Mr. Randall hadn't realized that closing his business would hurt more than just his own employees. The closing of Randall Manufacturing had affected the entire town. But some things couldn't be helped, and Gracie knew that the economy had played a role in Mr. Randall's decision.

Gracie coughed and searched quickly to make sure Patrick hadn't heard Lacey's question. "No, of course not. Listen, Lacey, I'm really busy. Can I help you with something?"

"Oh, yes, of course. I have these old cabinets that I want to spruce up."

"We have a textured spray paint that works great. Let me show you what I mean."

Lacey followed her to the paint section. "Can you show me how to use it? I can paint my nails, but anything more than that and I'm at a loss."

"Sure, I'll get plywood and show you how it works."

"You're a lifesaver, Gracie. And really, if I was you, I'd be head over heels in love with that Patrick Fogerty. If I had half a chance, I'd ask him over for dinner."

"Since you're single, Lacey, maybe you should invite him to the church social next week. He's a great guy. I can introduce you."

She looked around for her boss and saw him heading for the back room. If she didn't know better, she would call it running. Surely he hadn't heard her weak attempt to fix him up with Lacey?

Patrick was a great guy and he deserved to

marry someone nice, settle down in Bygones and raise a few kids. As for Gracie, she was done with everything white. It would be a long time before she decided to try romance again.

Chapter Three

At five-thirty, Patrick locked the door and switched the sign to Closed. He turned to watch Gracie straighten shelves that had been ransacked by curious customers who had done a lot of business in the store that day. His best day yet.

Thanks to Gracie, the Bygones Runaway Bride. That was what he'd heard people calling her and he'd overheard Whitney, the local reporter, discussing the headline for Thursday's paper. He needed to tell Gracie that she would soon be front-page news. He just didn't know how to bring it up.

If today had been bad for her, Thursday would be a nightmare.

She turned, saw him watching her and smiled. He found it a lot easier to smile back than he'd imagined. He'd been surprised by several things today. First and foremost, her lack of tears over the marriage that wasn't. Shouldn't she be crying? Wouldn't she be second-guessing herself?

He'd heard the "cold feet" theory floated by several people. Some said the wedding would take place in a month or so, after she had time to think about it.

"Hey, I've been thinking about something today." She turned from the cans of spray paint and wiped her hands on the apron that came to her knees because it was meant for a person a lot bigger than she was.

"What's that?"

"Workshops for women." Gracie looked around, as if she was still thinking up the plan.

"Workshops for women? What is that?"

"What you should do. What we could do to draw in customers. I don't know, I guess I've always had to do things for myself and I thought that all women—well, maybe not *all,* but most women—could figure things out for themselves. Today I learned that a lot of them don't have a clue. They can't even paint a cabinet with spray paint. One of them bought a precut bookshelf off the internet and she didn't know how to put it together or if she even had the tools."

"What are you getting at, Gracie?" Patrick slipped the apron off his neck and rolled up the sleeves he'd kept down and buttoned at his wrists during the workday.

"We could do workshops." She gave him a look that said the name was self-explanatory. "For women. We can teach them how to build a bookshelf, make their homes more secure or more energy efficient. And in the process, we could bring in business."

He looked around the little store that was his future, his dream, and then back to the woman who had maybe come up with an idea that would keep his future in the black. Lately he'd been taking on more handyman jobs just to keep things going. He'd also been considering going online with the store and with the rocking chairs he'd been building. Her idea would be one more thing to help make his store profitable.

"I like it, and I think you're definitely my new assistant manager."

She laughed and he was taken by surprise that her laughter made him smile. "You realize I'm your only employee, right?"

"I do realize that, but today you did the work of three people."

"And I managed, through one little wedding scandal, to bring in dozens of customers you hadn't expected."

"I hate to say it, but yes, you did."

Pink crawled up her neck into her cheeks. "I heard more personal stories today than I ever thought I'd hear. I never planned on being anyone's hero or the person everyone shared their tales of heartbreak with."

"I'm sure you didn't. And did you plan on trying to fix me up with half the single women in Bygones?" More pink. He laughed because it served her right. "I overheard you tell at least a dozen women that I'm single and the nicest guy you know and they should maybe ask me to the social, or the singles meeting, or even out for a cup of coffee."

"Oops. Well, you are single and nice, and if you're going to stay in Bygones, you should go out once in a while, not work all of the time."

"Thank you for thinking of me, Gracie, but I'll be fine. I can cook, do my own laundry and even put a bookcase together."

"I'm sure you can."

"Let's grab some coffee. We could both use a break."

"I should go home." She pulled the cell phone out of her pocket and glanced at the time. "I need to cook dinner, and my little brother has a load of laundry that he can't wash on his own."

"I think they'll be fine without you for a little

while. Who would have done those things for them if…"

He sighed and wished he'd kept his thoughts to himself. He didn't need to get this involved. What Gracie did for her family was none of his concern.

"If I'd gotten married?" She folded up her apron but held it in her hands, staring at it rather than looking at him.

"I imagine your little brother can do a load of laundry."

"I've been taking care of them for years, you know. I mean, I'll be twenty-five in October, and for almost fifteen years I've been cooking, doing their laundry, mending their clothes and stopping their fights. It's hard to let go."

He knew all about letting go. The words reminded him of the day he'd watched all the stock from the Fogerty Hardware store being loaded into a truck and shipped to a large store in a nearby community. He'd signed the building over to the new owner and he'd let go of a family business that he'd invested his life in. The same business his father had died in.

Until that day, he hadn't seen that he'd been heading down the same path as his father. The path of long hours, at least.

"Let's have that coffee." She looked up from

the apron she was still holding. "And maybe something to eat. I'm starving. My boss is a nice guy, but I barely had time for lunch today."

"That would be your fault. You're the one that left the groom at the altar and caused all this notoriety for yourself."

"True, very true, but you're the guy all the women in town are mooning over."

"I'm starting to think they need more single men in Bygones." He opened the door to the stockroom and watched as she gathered her purse and the lunch she hadn't eaten. "I have leftover chili if you're hungry."

"Chili that I didn't cook? That sounds great."

Great. He had offered. She had accepted. He led her outside and up the back steps to his apartment.

Gracie walked up the steps and through the door into the apartment over the hardware store. Her mouth dropped, seriously dropped. Patrick Fogerty was a genius. She knew how to repair a wall, build a porch and fix a roof, but what he'd done with that decades-old apartment was amazing.

"It's beautiful." She had seen it before he started working on it. It was a typical apartment from a building that had seen its heyday in the

1920s or earlier. The rooms had been small, the floors covered with teal carpet, and the plaster walls had been cracked and chipped.

Patrick stood back, pride evident on his ruggedly handsome face as she wandered through what had become a loft-style apartment. The rooms had been opened up, wood floors put down. The windows were open and a breeze blew in. The kitchen had sleek European-style cabinets in deep mahogany, and the lights were bar lights that focused on different areas of the open living room and kitchen area.

"I'm impressed. How did you come up with all this in Bygones?"

"I made a trip to Manhattan, Kansas, obviously, not New York. Or several trips. I found surplus cabinets and flooring for a great price. Since I do the labor myself, it didn't cost much."

"You could forget the hardware store and do this for a living."

"I enjoy the hardware store."

Gracie wandered into the kitchen and thought she'd love to cook in a kitchen like this one, with new appliances and sleek, modern fixtures. The kitchen at the farm hadn't been updated in years. The cookstove had to be lit with a match each time she used it. She had installed a new faucet and kept the oven working.

"Coffee?" Patrick pushed a button on the single-serve coffeemaker.

"Please." She wandered back to the living room. "I've lived on the farm my whole life and thought I'd always live on a farm until I met..." She sighed and turned to face Patrick, "Trent. We were going to live in Manhattan."

"I see."

He handed her a cup of coffee, and she took it and sat at the bar that separated the kitchen from the dining area and living room.

"I don't think I'd make a good lawyer's wife. It's too much pressure."

"I think you'd be fine."

She smiled at that and at the tone of his voice that said he was uncomfortable with the conversation. She understood. Two days ago she'd been engaged. Now she was sitting in Patrick's apartment discussing what would have been.

"I'm always fine, Patrick. It's how I'm wired. I deal with life and move on."

He sat down next to her, a steaming cup of coffee in front of him. "It isn't always that easy."

"No, I guess it isn't. But it makes people more comfortable if they think you're fine. If you smile when they ask how you are and tell them you're great, it makes them happy." She lifted the cup and took a sip because she was saying too much and no one really wanted to hear it. And she was too embarrassed to tell the whole truth.

She hadn't been good enough for Trent Morgan. No matter how she dressed up, fixed her hair and did all of the other girl stuff that Trent seemed to think was important, it hadn't been enough. He'd always been trying to change her, to make her fit the mold of who he wanted her to be.

She held the coffee cup in her hand and thought about how much she wanted to tell someone other than her dad what Trent had done to her, that he'd tried to change her, that he'd cheated on her. He hadn't loved her enough.

Someday she wanted to be loved enough.

"How about that chili?" Patrick left the seat next to her and she smiled as he opened the fridge door to pull out a bowl.

"I could make something if you don't want leftovers."

"I thought we'd agreed that you don't always have to take care of everyone?"

She started to nod but her phone rang. She pulled it out of her pocket and groaned. "Yes, that's what we agreed, but I have to take this." She answered. "What is it, Evan?"

Her younger brother responded, "Shouldn't you be home by now?"

"I should, but I'm still in town. What do you need?"

"There's nothing for supper and you said you'd throw my laundry in for me. I have to go to Oklahoma tomorrow."

"You can do laundry. I taught you how, remember? And there's a casserole in the freezer. Preheat the oven to four hundred degrees and bake it for an hour."

"Seriously? Where are you? Everyone is saying you flipped out Saturday. I'm starting to think they're right."

"Maybe I have. And maybe it's time you learned to take care of yourself." She wanted to tell him that if he'd bothered showing up for the wedding he wouldn't have to get second-hand information.

He hung up on her and she didn't know what to do. The microwave dinged and Patrick pulled a bowl out and set it in front of her.

"See, that wasn't so hard, now, was it?" He reached into a cabinet and handed her a package of crackers.

"It wasn't easy." She took the crackers and the spoon he handed her. "He really can't take care of himself."

"I'm sure he can, if he has to."

"Maybe." Gracie crunched a few crackers into her chili and leaned in to inhale the lovely aroma. "Do you have family, Patrick?"

"I have an older brother in California. My dad passed away several years ago. My mom remarried and lives in Georgia."

"I see." She watched as he moved around the kitchen, a confident man, terribly handsome. She focused, for some reason, on the sleeves of his plaid shirt that he'd rolled up to reveal strong, deeply tanned forearms.

He sat down next to her and she refocused on the bowl of chili.

"My family has a tendency to do their own thing," he said, handing her a package of shredded cheese.

"Mine like to be very involved in each other's lives."

"Isn't that part of being in a small town?"

She shrugged. "I guess. I don't know because it's all I've ever known. And taking care of my family is all I've ever known."

His hand settled on hers. "Eat your chili before you go rushing off to rescue your brother."

She closed her eyes and tried to find a reason why his command, the softness of his voice, would make her want to cry. Maybe it had to do with exhaustion catching up with her? The past six months of planning the wedding had felt like being tied to a race car and dragged around the track with no way to escape.

"It will get better," his voice continued, smooth and reassuring.

Gracie looked up at him, studying the handsome face, brown eyes the color of coffee with just enough cream. She blinked a few times to clear her thoughts. She somehow convinced herself it was that exhaustion thing again.

"Yes, it'll get better. But I should go."

"Of course." He started to say something but a knock on the door interrupted.

"And you have company."

"I wasn't expecting company."

"Another perk to living in a small town. Always expect company and usually when you least expect it." She finished the last bite of chili and carried the bowl to the sink.

Patrick watched her for a brief second and then he answered the repeated knock on the door. Gracie grabbed her purse and keys. When she walked around the corner, Patrick was standing in the doorway. Willa Douglas, single and pretty, stood on the landing with a casserole dish in her hands. Her eyes widened when she saw Gracie.

Gracie smiled at Willa and then at Patrick. "See you tomorrow, boss."

As Gracie hurried down the stairs, she told herself that what she felt wasn't disappointment or even jealousy. She'd had enough of men in her life. She definitely wasn't the type of person to have a rebound relationship just days after ending an engagement.

Patrick Fogerty was a decent man. Maybe even a friend. She liked that idea. He could be her friend. Friendship was easy and uncomplicated. A friend wouldn't break her heart.

Chapter Four

Early Wednesday morning, Patrick walked down the sidewalk with a steaming cup of coffee from the Cozy Cup Café. He'd been the first customer, and he and Josh Smith had talked shop. Josh needed some repairs to a door that someone had tried to open during the night. Patrick had questions about his store computer. Everything these days was computerized, even the cash register. For a guy that liked to hit a few buttons, have a drawer pop open and be done with it, it was hard to adjust.

The two of them had also talked about the upcoming block party that the store owners were organizing with Gracie's help. They would have door prizes and other programs to draw in business. But lately the biggest draw was one Gracie Wilson. The Bygones Runaway Bride, as she'd been renamed, was bringing in more business than anyone could have expected.

Who knew that people would be that curious about a woman standing up a man at the altar?

He paused as he crossed Bronson Avenue. Of course, there was no traffic at this early hour. In the distance he heard trucks at the Wilsons' granary and he could see a car or two coming up Main Street, probably to get something at the Sweet Dreams Bakery. He had considered stopping in but he needed to get down to his store and do some last-minute stocking before he opened the doors.

As he continued down the sidewalk, past the freshly painted brick buildings that the town seemed to be having a hard time accepting, he thought about the conversation he and Josh had just had about the benefactor of the town, the person responsible for funding the face-lift of the downtown area and the money for the new businesses.

The speculation had turned to Robert Randall, owner of the recently closed Randall Manufacturing. Maybe the old guy had felt guilty for what he'd done to the town, closing the plant and all. That had been Patrick's thought lately.

Patrick sipped the best cup of coffee he'd had in a long time and slowed to look in the store windows. He passed his shop and looked in the window of the Fluff & Stuff pet store. He'd been thinking lately that it would be nice to have a dog. He hadn't had a pet since his teen years. He'd just been too busy for anything other than himself.

His family hadn't been pet people, anyway. They'd traveled. They'd worked. His parents had ignored each other.

Behind him he heard a shrill voice calling, "Yoo-hoo, Patrick."

He turned and smiled at Ann Mars as she crossed the road, her long white hair stacked on her head in a knot that seemed to continuously slip to one side. She was a tiny thing, and he always had a strange urge to pick her up and set her on something so he wouldn't have to lean to talk to her. He smiled at the thought. She was a dynamo and would probably swat his hands if he tried anything like that.

"Miss Mars, good morning."

"Hello to you, too, Patrick, and don't call me Miss Mars. My goodness, you are a tall drink of water." She craned her neck to look up at him.

"I am?" He took a sip of his coffee and waited.

"I thought I'd check with you to see how our Gracie is doing."

Our Gracie? He cleared his throat and started

to object, but he didn't. He was learning to be small town, and he knew that if he tried to deny Gracie, he'd be in serious trouble. She might have left Trent Morgan at the altar, but to these sweet ladies, both Ann Mars and Coraline Connolly, Gracie seemed to be the victim. They probably knew more about the situation than he did.

"She seems to be surviving the uproar, Ann."

"That's because she survives, Patrick. She's survived everything." She hooked her arm through his. "Walk with me."

"Yes, ma'am."

"She's survived losing her mother. She has survived that rowdy bunch of men in her home. She's cooked, cleaned and taken care of everything since she was just a little girl. She's going to handle this situation, too. She's going to do what she always does. She's going to hold her chin up and take care of everyone. And she isn't going to let on that she's hurting at all."

"I see." He pulled the store key from his pocket as they made their way back up the street to his store. His store. He admired the light-colored brick, the windows painted simply with The Fixer-Upper and the green awning over the wide glass-and-wood door. He turned his attention back to the tiny woman at his side, smiling down at her. "She has good friends. I know you and Miss Coraline will help her through this."

"And so we will. But you're going to have to keep an eye on her while she's here. People are circling like buzzards after roadkill, and if that Morgan woman hasn't showed up, she will."

"I'll do my best."

He unlocked the door, and Ann Mars stared up at him, her mouth twisted and her eyes scrunched nearly closed. "Patrick Fogerty, you're a gentleman and I'm counting on you."

He thought that this was the place in the conversation where someone would hand him a manila envelope and tell him his assignment, should he wish to accept it, was inside. But Gracie Wilson wasn't his assignment. He had a business that needed his attention. He had a new life here in Bygones, and it was already complicated enough without the SOS committee becoming the Save Gracie Foundation.

He doubted very seriously that Gracie Wilson wanted him as a bodyguard. He'd been around town long enough to know she had five overprotective brothers who took their duties seriously. She'd complained in the past that they could be a little overwhelming at times.

"Ann, I'm not convinced that Gracie and

Trent won't work things out. Maybe the wedding will still take place."

"Why in the world would you think that?"

"Because people get cold feet."

Ann pursed her lips again, a sure sign that he wasn't saying what she wanted to hear. "Gracie doesn't run from anything."

He pushed the door open. "I should get in here and get things ready to start the day."

"And I need to get back up the street to my place," Ann Mars replied.

"I'll see you later."

He watched as she marched away, her arms swinging as she hurried off toward This 'N' That. For a woman in her eighties, she had a lot of energy. He smiled, shook his head and stepped inside the hardware store.

As he walked through the store, he stopped to flip on lights. He turned on the cash register and checked to make sure the coffeepot had started brewing. A car honked outside. He turned and watched as a dog walked slowly across the street and then down the sidewalk. The animal, a medium-size brown mutt with wiry hair, had been around for a few days. He thought maybe someone had dumped it in hopes the Fluff & Stuff pet store would take the animal in.

He liked dogs as much as anyone, but the

mixed breed with wiry brown hair and floppy ears seemed to think the best place to hang out was the front door of The Fixer-Upper. Since it had started hanging around Bygones, he would often find it curled up on the sidewalk in front of his store.

The front door opened and the bell chimed to announce a customer. He glanced at his watch and started to tell the woman entering the store that he wasn't open yet. But she didn't look like a woman he wanted to argue with. Her short hair was perfectly cut. Her suit, a skirt, jacket and blouse, looked expensive. And she looked angry.

"Where is she?" The woman marched down the aisle between the saws and drills, her mouth a tight line of disapproval.

"I'm sorry?" He reached for the dark green work apron he wore in the store.

"Gracie Wilson. Where is she?"

And then it hit him. Mrs. Morgan. Lovely woman. He wondered why the dog hadn't barked. A good dog would have barked a warning.

"She isn't here yet."

"When do you expect her?"

He glanced at his watch and caught the groan before it slipped out. "Soon."

"Then I'll wait."

He caught sight of an old farm truck and he knew that Gracie would soon walk through the back door. The dog out front seemed to be waiting for her. It stood, wagging a wiry brush of a tail. That confirmed his suspicions that the dog might be getting fed here at the store.

"Maybe if you come back later it would be better." He took the woman by the arm, nearly choking on the cloud of perfume that clung to the air around her.

"I need to speak to Miss Wilson because there is the small matter of what she owes me."

The front door opened again. Patrick didn't know if he should breathe a sigh of relief or pray for mercy. A hardware store, at least the one he'd grown up in, was a man's world. He knew about building things, fixing things. He didn't know about small-town politics, drama and what appeared to be women on the warpath.

Coraline Connolly marched down the aisle, her nose in the air and her pace brisk. She wasn't a big woman, but she walked with the authority of a woman who had been a school principal and knew how to handle problems.

"Mrs. Morgan, my goodness, imagine seeing you here." Coraline smiled a frozen smile that Patrick was pretty glad he wasn't the recipient of.

"Coraline, this has nothing to do with you."

Coraline moved Patrick aside. "Oh, I know that. I just thought the two of us could take a little walk. We have some fund-raisers coming up in town and I'd love to be able to put your family name on the list of benefactors."

"I need to speak to Gracie." Mrs. Morgan pulled her arm from Coraline's grasp.

"I'm sure you do, but I have other appointments and you are so great at organizing events. I'll buy you a cup of coffee," Coraline offered. "I'm sure Gracie will be here by the time we're finished."

Mrs. Morgan glanced around the store and finally sighed, giving in to Coraline. Patrick watched as the mother of Trent Morgan was escorted from the store.

"Is it safe?" Gracie walked through the door, peeking around the store for any sign of the woman who, had things been different, would have been her mother-in-law.

Patrick walked to the front of the store and looked out the window. "For now."

"Good." She slipped her work apron over her head. "I'm going to have to face her eventually."

"Probably."

Gracie tied her apron and reached for a coffee

cup. "I'm sorry this is becoming your problem. It shouldn't be. I'll talk to her. I need to give the dress back, and maybe that will start the road to making things better."

Giving the dress back would be a step toward making this real. She obviously couldn't explain that to her boss; the man seemed pretty uncomfortable with the conversation.

"Are you sure you don't want to think about this before giving the dress back?"

The coffee overflowed on her hand. She pulled back, reaching quickly for a napkin to wipe her scalded hand and then the drops of brown on the floor. She glanced up at Patrick as she straightened to throw the napkin away.

"I'm positive I don't want that dress or a chance to think."

He shrugged and let it go, handing her a wet wipe for her hand rather than commenting further.

"I stopped at the *Gazette* and put the ad in for the Workshops for Women." She shifted topics because she was tired of the current subject. Trent. It was time to move on. The workshops would be a great way to bring in customers. And it gave them something to talk about other than the wedding.

"That's good, thank you." He glanced at his

watch and groaned. "Will you be okay here for an hour or so? I got a call last night from a woman who needs a light installed."

"Did you?" She smiled because even though she was done with romance, that didn't mean everyone should be. At her church's ladies' meeting last night she'd told Annabelle to give Patrick a call, because he had to be the greatest catch in Bygones.

"I did." He had started toward the front door but he turned. "Why is it you don't seem surprised?"

She thought about avoiding answering. Instead she smiled her best innocent smile and told the truth. "Because last night a friend mentioned needing a light installed and I told her you do great work."

"Thanks, I think."

Gracie ignored the growing lump in her throat because in the shadows she saw something on his face, a sadness, or loss. It had to be her imagination. And maybe the way her heart shook a little was her imagination, too.

"Would it help if I said she's pretty and very sweet?"

"Not really." He cleared his throat. "Gracie, I'm really not looking for someone."

"No one ever is. Sometimes the right person

happens into our lives when we're least expecting it."

"Happens. As in, they come along unexpectedly, not because everyone in town is helping it to happen."

She laughed a little and felt the lump dissolve because his smile had reappeared. "Isn't it great living in a small town?"

He flipped on the open sign and headed back in her direction. She felt that tightness in her throat again. He was tall and broad-shouldered, his dark hair always looking a little messy. Last night one of the ladies at the church meeting asked why Gracie wanted to push such a handsome man off on someone else. Gracie had to admit she didn't have a clue. Self-preservation maybe?

"Oh, I also submitted information about the block party on Main Street. Coraline said it would be great for the school to put together fund-raisers, maybe baked goods, candles, that type of stuff."

"Changing the subject?" He pulled off his apron and tossed it on the counter.

The door chimed. Saved by the bell. She exhaled and grinned up at her boss. "Not at all, just filling you in on everything."

"Do you have a list I should know about? Ad

for workshops. Check. Article about block party. Check. Get Patrick married off. Check."

"Something like that. I can give you a full list later."

"Thanks, I'd appreciate that." He grinned and pulled keys out of his pocket. "Does she have the light fixture or do I need to take one?"

"She has it." She grabbed a piece of paper off the counter and wrote out the address. "Here you go."

"I'm not sure if I'm going to thank you for this."

"You will."

He left and Gracie turned her attention to the customer at the front of the store. She smiled at Mr. Fibley, once the pharmacist in town. Now that the drugstore had closed, he spent his days at the bookstore and sometimes visiting Ann Mars at This 'N' That. He was a dapper little man with a sweet smile.

"Mr. Fibley, what can I help you with?"

He looked around the store. "I haven't been in here yet and I really thought I ought to come check it out."

"Oh, I see." Gracie shoved her hands into the loose pockets of the apron and waited.

"I thought I might need lightbulbs. Do you carry lightbulbs?"

"We do. What kind do you need?"

"Oh, those expensive energy savers, I suppose. My niece told me they last forever."

"They do last awhile." She took him by the arm and they walked through the store to the aisle with bulbs and other home items.

"Are you doing okay, Gracie?" he asked, leaning in to whisper when they reached the light-bulbs.

Gracie smiled and nodded, but she couldn't answer because his kindness caused an immediate tightness in her throat and a sudden sting of tears behind her eyes.

He patted her arm. "I know that people are being hard on you, but you'll get through this. I've watched you grow up and you've always been a fighter."

"Thank you, Mr. Fibley."

"There, those are the lightbulbs." He laughed a little as he reached for two boxes. "And you thought I just came in here to stick my nose in your business. You know, people ought to be shopping local. Prices might be a little higher, but with the price of gas, it doesn't make sense to drive to the city for things we can get right here."

"I agree, Mr. Fibley. Hopefully, we can convince people that we're right."

They walked back to the register and Gracie rang up the lightbulbs. Mr. Fibley took the paper bag and gave her another sweet smile.

"You'll be just fine, Gracie Wilson."

"Thank you, sir."

He winked and then he left, taking slow steps, examining the store as he went. At the door he stopped to admire bird feeders, and then, with a wave back at her, he walked out the door.

A few minutes later she heard the rumble of a motorcycle. She walked to the front of the store and peeked out. The dog she'd been feeding for the past few days looked up from his place on the doormat and wagged his tail. She'd brought a food and water bowl today and she'd fed him at the back door. He seemed nice enough and didn't even bother to get up when people walked past. Maybe he should have a name if he was going to stick around? She'd have to think about that.

She opened the door and reached to pet his wiry head. He licked her hand and then lost interest. A few parking spaces down from the store, she spotted her brother Evan getting off his bike. He hooked the helmet over the handlebar and raked a hand through his unruly dark hair. Sunglasses hid the black eye he'd gotten the previous day when a bull tossed him and then slammed a horn into his cheek.

"What are you doing here?" she asked as he walked up the sidewalk.

"Came to check on my big sister."

"Really?" She opened the door and walked back inside. Evan followed. The dog returned to the mat.

"I do care."

He spotted the coffeepot and poured himself a cup of the steaming brew that couldn't begin to compete with the coffee at the Cozy Cup Café. But they weren't in competition. They just wanted to offer people a cup of coffee while they browsed. The farmers liked it because they sometimes wanted to stand around and talk before heading back to work.

"This is bad coffee." He took a careful sip and made a face.

"It's free."

"Right." He put the cup down on the counter. "Trent Morgan came by the house this morning looking for you. I guess he's postponed his trip a couple of days. You know, the honeymoon?"

"I know."

"Are you going to work things out with him?"

"No."

"So this wasn't just cold feet or anything."

She picked up the cup of coffee he had abandoned and took a sip. "No, and if you'd been home, you would have known that."

"I couldn't miss that rodeo."

"No, of course you couldn't." She tried to blink away the tears, because her brother skipping her wedding, even if the wedding hadn't happened, still hurt.

"I wasn't about to come watch you hitch up with a guy you didn't love."

"Why did you think that?"

Evan shrugged one shoulder and took the cup back. "That's my coffee. And you didn't love Trent Morgan. You were trying to be everyone's hero again. You accepted his proposal and then you got to know him better and realized he wasn't the guy you thought. But you couldn't back out when everyone was planning that wedding and counting on you. Give it up, Gracie. Stop always doing the right thing. It makes the rest of us look bad."

He said the last with a smile that didn't settle in his dark eyes, didn't lighten the mood.

"I obviously don't always do the right thing. Remember, I sneaked out the window at my own wedding and left Trent at the altar."

"Smartest thing you've ever done, sis."

She stood on tiptoe and Evan leaned in so

she could kiss his cheek. "You're a mess but I love you."

Under his dark tan, he turned a little red. "Yeah, I love you, too. And now for the other reason I'm here."

"What's that?"

"Dad."

"Okay." She waited, holding her breath.

"I know he's real worried about the granary, and now Mrs. Morgan is telling everyone we owe her big."

"I'll take care of that. Dad doesn't have to worry. And you don't have to worry about Dad."

"I'm not worried about the old man."

"Yes, you are."

Evan didn't respond. He didn't smile or agree. As he turned to walk away, Gracie reached for his arm.

"I have to go, Gracie."

"I know, but not before I give you a hug. Please be safe this weekend."

"I'm always safe. And you aren't my mom."

She bit down on her lip and nodded. "No, I guess I'm not."

He hugged her and then he left. She walked to the front of the store and watched as he buckled on the helmet and started the bike. The engine roared to life, startling a couple of ladies walking down the sidewalk. She saw her brother grin and knew that behind the visor of this helmet he probably winked at the younger woman.

She glanced at her watch and wondered how things were going for Patrick. That made her smile, thinking of Patrick and her plans to help him find a wife. He needed to settle down and stay in Bygones.

It was a good plan, and yet, it made her feel empty inside.

Chapter Five

It was nearly closing time. Patrick looked at his watch and at the customer Gracie had been helping for the past thirty minutes. They'd had steady business all afternoon since he got back from helping the very single and looking Annabelle Clark. He couldn't thank Gracie for the setup.

Annabelle turned out to be a sweet woman of about thirty. She enjoyed cooking and taking her dogs for long walks in the park. As he installed the light, he was held hostage while she listed off information that made it sound as if she was providing personal details for a dating website.

He should have listed his own details. Patrick Fogerty, thirty-four and single with no interest in random dating. He'd yet to meet a woman who made him consider marriage. His parents' brutal divorce had been a life lesson he'd never forgot-

ten. Marriage should be more than two people
joined in holy matrimony but living separate
lives with three kids somewhere in the middle.

Gracie. He watched as she walked next to
the customer, an older woman he remembered
from church. Mrs. Duncan. She baked cookies
for visitors to the Bygones Community Church
and sometimes liked to sit in the rocking chairs
that Patrick made. He usually kept one or two
on the sidewalk in front of the store.

As he started closing out the register for the
day, Gracie grabbed a few paintbrushes for Mrs.
Duncan. He couldn't hear what they were saying but he could tell Gracie seemed to be trying to talk her customer out of something. Or
into something.

They continued down the aisle, getting closer
to the counter. He smiled as he listened.

"Mrs. Duncan, I really can't sell you a ladder," Gracie said, holding their customer's arm
as they walked. "It wouldn't be safe."

"Well, Gracie Wilson, you know I don't have
children. And I certainly can't pay someone. It's
just that the town is looking so nice and clean,
but my old house, well, it's like a stain on a new
dress."

"Mrs. Duncan, your house is beautiful." Gracie said it so earnestly Patrick had to smile.

"It hasn't been painted in twenty years, Gracie. Now, I might be getting on in years, but I can still see."

"I'll paint your house." Gracie put the brushes and other supplies on the counter. "You tell me what color and we'll go ahead and ring up the paint. I'm off tomorrow and we close early on Saturday. Maybe I can get my brothers to help."

"I can't ask you to paint my house."

Gracie kissed the older woman on the cheek. Patrick watched as the two women, both obviously strong-willed, continued to argue.

"You're not asking, Mrs. Duncan. I'm offering." Gracie said it as if that was the end of the argument.

Patrick sighed, because he knew where this argument would land him. By the end of the week he'd be on a ladder, painting. Because Gracie had a way of dragging other people along. The block party at the end of the month. The rocking chairs she'd encouraged him to make, and now her obvious plan to marry him off. He drew the line on that one.

But helping Mrs. Duncan paint her house, that he wouldn't mind doing. He'd come to Bygones looking for slower pace, a shorter workweek and the closeness of a small town. He thought he might get everything but the shorter workweek.

"Mrs. Duncan, I'll help Gracie. I bet if we

find some volunteers, we can paint your house in just a day or two." Patrick smiled at Gracie and Mrs. Duncan as he made the offer.

Mrs. Duncan smiled big. "Well, now, aren't you two the sweetest couple?"

"Oh, we're not…" Gracie's mouth opened and she turned a little pale.

"Gracie, everyone in town is talking about you and that wedding you didn't show up for. There had to be a good reason, and now I can see what it was."

"Mrs. Duncan, I'm only Gracie's employer." He smiled at Gracie. "And her friend."

"Of course." Mrs. Duncan pulled cash out of her purse. "Here's what I have. Do you think that's enough to cover the paint?"

Patrick took the money and counted it. It wouldn't begin to cover the cost of paint. He handed it back to the woman. "I'll bill you when we're finished, since we don't know how much the paint will cost."

"Now, I can't afford much more than that." She shoved the money back into her wallet.

"It won't be more." Patrick bagged up the brushes. "I'll keep the supplies here so we have them when we start painting."

Mrs. Duncan smiled. "That is so nice. I might buy some of those mums you have outside, too. And a flag for my front porch."

"We'll make sure we bring them with us."
Gracie smiled back at Patrick as she led her customer toward the front door.

Patrick watched as the two women walked down the sidewalk, the stray dog following close behind. The dog's tail wagged and he knew that Gracie was the reason the animal wouldn't leave. When he'd come back earlier, he'd seen the food bowl in the alley behind his store. He shook his head and went back to work, closing out the register for the night.

A few minutes later Gracie returned. She looked a little hesitant as she stood on the opposite side of the counter.

"I take it you haven't heard that rumor?" She fiddled with the desk calendar and didn't look at him.

"That was a new one." He zipped up the bank-deposit bag and cleared his throat. "They'll have something new to talk about by the end of the month."

"Maybe I should start a rumor?" She smiled up at him, her darks eyes twinkling, either from humor or unshed tears. He didn't see Gracie Wilson as the type of woman to spend too much time crying over something she couldn't change.

"I think someone else will take care of it for you."

"I hope so. Cold feet, another man, an argument over money and, my favorite, that I couldn't take much more of his mother."

"That one sounds like the winner."

She laughed at that. "I kept telling myself I was marrying Trent, not his mother, in the end." She shrugged. "Hey, Josh has coffee and Melissa has day-old pastries. They're sitting down at the end of the block on lawn chairs and they wanted to know if we'd like to join them. An impromptu meeting or maybe just an excuse to visit and drink coffee. I'm invited because they want to talk about the Main Street Block Party at the end of the month."

"Sounds like a plan. Let me finish up here while you feed your dog and we'll head that way."

"That is not my dog." Her dark brows arched and she seemed to try an innocent look, but the expression broke down midway and she laughed. "Okay, I've been feeding him."

"I thought so."

"I could take him to the farm but my dad told me no more strays."

"He can stay here. We'll build him a doghouse and put it under the stairs that lead up to my place." He had to be crazy for offering, but he'd gotten attached to the stray and had fed it a few times himself. "You might want to name him so we can stop calling him 'the dog.'"

"You're a nice guy, Patrick Fogerty."

"Don't let it get around."

She followed him to the stockroom. "I'm afraid people are already catching on."

He turned to say something but she was right behind him and they nearly collided. He caught her arms to keep her from running into him and she looked up, her smile disappearing. Patrick released her slowly, a little too slowly for good sense. Her arms had been soft under his hands; her hair smelled like a tropical island.

He'd never loved the tropics, but suddenly he was tempted. It took him by surprise.

"Sorry," she whispered and backed away a step. "I wasn't paying attention."

"No, me, neither." He made a pretense of grabbing his jacket and a couple of lawn chairs. "I'll go lock the front door."

She nodded and hurried away. Patrick watched her go. He leaned the lawn chairs against the wall and headed back to the front door to make sure it was locked. He needed those few minutes to get his head on straight, because after years of self-control, he couldn't afford to let go now. He needed to focus on his business and Gracie was his employee. She was also a woman who had just ended an engagement.

Good reasons for not getting involved.

The dog followed them down the block to the front of the Cozy Cup Café, where several people were sitting together. There were lawn chairs, folding tables and the bench that had been installed during the refurbishing of downtown Bygones. Melissa Sweeney, owner of the Sweet Dreams Bakery, and Brian Montclair, her fiancé, were sitting on the bench, cozy and in love. An unlikely couple, everyone had said. But Gracie didn't think so.

She'd known Brian forever and she was so glad he'd found someone as sweet as Melissa.

She smiled at Lily Farnsworth, owner of the new flower shop, Love in Bloom. Lily had been so sweet to Gracie during the pre-wedding fiasco, which had included Trent's mother trying to make every decision. Lily and Tate Bronson would soon be married. She wished them all the best and she could see that what they had was real and lasting.

The thought took her by surprise because it brought another thought. Had she ever felt that way about Trent? Had they looked at each other that way?

The others were gathered around. Joshua Smith, owner of the Cozy Cup Café, walked out of his store with two carafes of coffee. He handed one of the coffeepots to Allison True, owner of the Happy Endings Bookstore, and set the other on a table. He went back into the store and returned with a stack of foam cups.

Gracie unfolded her chair next to Chase Rollins, owner of the Fluff & Stuff pet shop, where she'd bought the supplies for the dog that seemed to have taken up residence at The Fixer-Upper. The dog that sadly needed a name.

"Is there anything I can do?" She looked around the group. She wasn't a store owner, but since they'd invited her, she decided to make the most of it.

"Just relax for a while, Gracie." Allison smiled happily as she handed out cups.

Josh poured coffee into Gracie's. "Have you followed up with Whitney at the *Gazette* concerning the article about the block party and the advertising?"

"Yes. And we both agree that we should go from the angle that people in the tri-county area should support local businesses. With the price of gas, it's cheaper to shop local, keep the money local, and support our local schools, police and fire departments."

Chase Rollins stood and moved his chair. Gracie gave him a curious look and he pointed. She glanced back and realized he was making space for Patrick. Heat climbed up her cheeks as everyone looked at the two of them. She thought about a quick disclaimer that they weren't a couple. She'd learned her lesson with Trent and she was officially off the dating scene for the time being.

But Patrick wasn't Trent Morgan and to say something would be to insult his integrity. She made quick eye contact with Allison, who smiled and went back to the subject of the block party.

"I think that's a great idea, Gracie." Allison reached for a pastry as she spoke. "I'm glad you're a part of this group. We need local input as well as the input of the new shop owners."

"We have a lot at stake." Chase leaned forward in his chair, a cup of steaming coffee in his hand. "If we don't make it, we've lost two years. Or less, I guess, if we can't make it that long. Someone invested a lot of money in this town and we owe it to them, to the SOS folks and to the community to give this our best shot."

"My thoughts exactly." Melissa handed her the tray of pastries from her bakery.

Gracie took one and handed the tray to Patrick. She looked up, meeting only kindness in his dark eyes. Her heart ached a little and she knew that was only natural. Less than a week had passed; she knew it would hurt for a while. Trent had stolen her trust. He had broken her heart, although that had happened long before the wedding. And now Trent looked like the victim.

Only she and her dad knew the truth. She had shared with her dad so that he wouldn't think the worst of her and because she needed one person on her side when everyone else in town was discussing how she'd walked away from a marriage to the perfect man.

When she looked up, Lily was watching, her look a combination of sympathy and curiosity. Joshua moved to his seat. Gracie focused on his words as he started to speak but her attention focused on his mouth. He had one of those smiles that sometimes took her by surprise. She didn't quite know why. Maybe because at times his smile seemed familiar.

She'd once been told she had one of those faces, the kind that often got mistaken for someone's niece, a granddaughter, someone familiar. Joshua probably got the same comments from people.

"One key to success is to keep coming up

with products our customers can't get anywhere else, or not easily. We can also give them service that they're not going to find in bigger department stores." Joshua leaned forward in his chair, earnest and committed to his store and to the rest of the new businesses in town. "Like Patrick's added handyman services."

Gracie glanced at Patrick, wanting him to mention painting Mrs. Duncan's home. He shifted in his chair and inclined his head in her direction.

"You tell them." He smiled a little and lifted his cup of coffee.

"I'm not really a member of this team."

Lily cleared her throat. "I think you're close enough. You came up with the idea for the block party. You're very important to us because you're our local tie."

"Gracie, if you're getting us into something…" Allison, who had known her years ago, laughed a little.

"Okay, this is my thought. We've put a lot into refurbishing Main Street. We're rebuilding our economy so that we can keep our school and our police and fire departments. But we've maybe neglected the rest of our town. Mrs. Duncan came in today. She was going to try to paint her own house because she wants it to look as nice as Main Street." She indicated the improved downtown with the new streetlights, the potted evergreens and the pretty stores. "She'd like her house painted, a flag and maybe flowers. She can't afford the improvements. And she obviously isn't physically capable of painting her own home."

"So you'd like to get volunteers and funds to help with a project that would beautify some of the older homes?" Joshua nodded and looked around the group.

"I think it's a great idea, Gracie." Melissa clasped her hands together, obviously all in on the idea. "So how do we get the funds?"

"I can get the paint, flags and fall mums at wholesale," Patrick offered. "We have three weeks until the block party. If we can get several groups of volunteers, we could possibly take care of four homes before the end of the month. That's being optimistic."

"I think optimism is what we need," Melissa said with a smile, glancing not at the group but at Brian.

"And faith." Lily smiled at Gracie. "It seems that lately every step we take is a step of faith. We have to believe that God brought us all together for a reason. Yes, with someone else's money, but I think there's a higher plan at work."

"Of course there is." Patrick looked around the group. "If I have your cooperation, I'll also bring this up at church to see if we can get more volunteers. Maybe we can get more than one team and we can work on more than one house at a time."

"I'll mention it at my church, too," Gracie offered. She glanced at her watch. "And now I have to go."

Gracie picked up her chair and finished her coffee, throwing her trash in the receptacle next to the door of Joshua's Cozy Cup Café. She looked around the group, because they were watching her, and watching Patrick, who had also stood.

"I'll walk you to your car." He took the chair she had in her hand. "See you all later. Let me know if there's anything else."

"I think we've taken care of a lot tonight. We'll keep planning the block party and get a list of volunteers for the home-beautification projects. Oh, and the media idea, to see if we can get coverage for the block party. They should love a 'small town trying to survive' story." Joshua stood and extended a hand to Patrick.

Gracie started down the sidewalk. The dog had been sleeping next to her chair, and he got lazily to his feet and trotted along next to her, his brown tail brushing the air. She reached down to pat his head and he looked up at her with adoring eyes, his tongue lolling from his open mouth. Adoration. A person could always count on a dog for being loyal and adoring.

"Hey, wait up," Patrick called out.

She glanced back and watched as he caught up with long strides. He smiled an easy, open smile. Gracie turned to keep walking because her mind couldn't process the reaction of her heart to this man. Not now, when she often felt bruised and broken.

Someday she would trust again, because she knew not all men cheated. But today felt too soon for trusting or even for what felt like a high-school crush of mega proportions. And she'd been out of high school for a long time.

"You didn't have to leave," she offered as they rounded the corner of the building at the end of the block. Her truck was parked in the alley behind the row of stores that faced Main Street.

"I need to get some work done." He walked with her to her old farm truck. "Are you heading home?"

She looked at the dog, who had decided to hop onto the back of her truck. "Rufus, you can't go with me."

"Rufus?" Patrick smiled at the dog and then at her.

"He needed a name." She reached up to pet the dog's wiry coat. Someone had mentioned that he looked as if he might be part Airedale. She thought he was smaller than that breed, and he was dark brown with no black or tan like an Airedale. But the wiry coat was like that of an Airedale.

Patrick reached for the dog's new collar, and it jumped to the ground.

"I'll keep an eye on him. Rufus." He shook his head as he said the dog's new name.

"Thank you. And I'm going home to help my dad with paperwork for the granary. He's trying to get a grant that will help offset some of the loss he's incurred in the last two years. With the drought piled on top of the economy, he's struggling."

"If I could help…"

She placed a hand on his arm but she couldn't meet his gaze, because it would be tender, full of sympathy, the look of a friend. "I know. And you are helping. You've hired me full-time."

"That's a no-brainer, Gracie. You bring in customers. You have an expertise very few workers would have."

"You'd be lost without me." She regretted the

silly words as soon as they slipped from her mouth. "I'm sorry."

"I would definitely be lost without you."

The air stilled and Gracie got lost for a moment in his words, in thinking what it would be like to be loved by a man like Patrick, by Patrick. A man who took care of stray dogs and volunteered to help a widow paint her home. What would it be like to have a man look at her the way Tate looked at Lily?

She knew that her raw emotions were still based on what had happened, not what was happening now.

"I should go." She reached to open the truck door but his hand was already there. Their fingers touched and Gracie moved as he opened the door for her.

"See you in the morning."

"Yes, in the morning." She climbed into the truck. He closed the door and she waved before cranking the old engine to life.

As she drove away, she saw him in her rearview mirror. She watched him stand next to the stairs that led up to his loft apartment. He stood there until she reached the end of the alley and then he started up the stairs, Rufus following along behind him.

Two years ago she'd met Trent at a Bygones

Community Church Christmas Bazaar. He'd sold her an old lamp and then he'd asked her out. He'd charmed her with compliments, gifts and promises of a perfect future. She'd fallen in love, or maybe she'd loved the idea of loving him.

She brushed at tears, angry that she still cried when she thought about his cheating on her. She had loved him but somewhere along the way the relationship had changed. It changed long before she knew that he cheated.

It changed because she started to realize she didn't fit the role he needed her to play. When they attended dinners he would criticize her appearance, her hair, her lack of makeup.

The thought brought another rush of emotion, mostly anger with herself for allowing Trent to do that to her.

She drove out of town, past the granary, past fields of drying sunflowers and corn that had been harvested. A few miles more and then she turned onto the gravel road that led to her family farm. They grew corn and wheat, but they also raised cattle. Her dad had always believed in diversifying. He held on to faith, even in the toughest times. He tried to stay out of debt.

He was a good man who had stayed in church and raised his children in church. She sometimes wondered why things had to be so hard for him. In the past when she had voiced those thoughts, he reminded her that God walked with them, even in the hard times. *The Lord is my Shepard. I shall not want.* He had made her learn Psalm 23 and as a child they often said it together, a reminder of God's faithfulness.

In the distance she saw her dad walk out of the barn. He took off his hat and swiped a hand across his forehead. Her brother Caleb joined him. The two talked for a minute and then Caleb headed for his truck.

She pulled her truck to a stop next to the house and got out. Their cow dog, a border collie named Sissy, ran to greet her. She ruffled the dog's soft black-and-white fur and smiled as her dad walked across the lawn. Sissy followed, sniffing at her legs, smelling the stray dog.

"Hi, Dad."

"Gracie, how's my girl today?" He kissed the top of her head and she wrapped an arm around his waist as they walked toward the back door of the house.

"I'm good, Dad. Did you get those financial records for me to go over for the grant?"

"I did. But you don't have to do that yet. We have a few weeks."

"I can do it now. What's up?"

Her dad paused at the back door of the house. He looked away and she studied his face, thinking he was still handsome and he should find someone to love. He'd been busy with his kids, he'd always said, and too busy to date.

"Dad?"

"Trent Morgan came by today."

"What did he have to say?"

"I don't know. I didn't give him much of a chance to talk." He grinned and motioned her inside. "I told him you were better off without a man that wouldn't be faithful."

"Dad, I really…"

"I'm your dad. I'm not going to let Trent Morgan show up here and try to pretend this is all about him. His mother has wagged her tongue all over town, talking about the money she spent. And people are talking about you running out on someone as upstanding as Trent."

"I know."

"But you aren't going to defend yourself. So I'll defend you. You're my girl and I'm not going to let them drag you through the dirt."

"Thanks, Dad." She reached for his big hand and he gave hers a good squeeze. "I'll make biscuits and gravy for dinner if you'd like."

"Not tonight, Gracie. I have—" He turned a little red. "I have a meeting."

"A meeting? Since when does a meeting make you turn red?"

He grinned, "The last I checked, I'm a grown man."

"Right, of course. Enjoy your date."

Her dad on a date. Her heart did a little lift and she smiled. Thirty minutes later, showered, changed and wearing cologne, he left and she stood at the door watching, probably the way he'd watched her go on dates over the years. She felt a little sentimental, a little worried, a little bit happy.

Emotions tumbled inside her. If things had been different, she would have been living in a pretty house on the edge of Manhattan, Kansas, not here in Bygones. She would have been Mrs. Trent Morgan. She would have been cooking dinner in her own kitchen, waiting for Trent to come home from work.

Waiting and wondering if he was really in a meeting or if he was with the pretty secretary she'd caught him with. She sighed, because not marrying him had been the right thing to do. Someday she'd find someone to love her. Someone who wouldn't let her down. Someone who would let her be herself, not try to change her into his ideal wife.

She was Gracie Wilson, farm girl, hardware-store employee and a person with faith to get her through hard times. She belonged in this town, with people who accepted her for who she was.

An image flashed through her mind of Patrick Fogerty. He accepted her for herself.

Chapter Six

Workshops for Women. Patrick had approved this idea, so he'd deal with the fallout. There were a half-dozen women in his store. His employee seemed to be their fearless leader and the person responsible for a renewed interest in his bachelor status.

Gracie Wilson. She moved through the group, showing them how to sand an old cabinet and then apply a coat of stain. At the next meeting she would work with them on step two.

She looked his way and smiled. He started to turn but instead he smiled back. She'd been quiet since the day of the impromptu meeting at the Cozy Cup Café. Today she'd come to work with circles under her eyes, as if she hadn't been sleeping. If a person needed a smile, a friend, it was Gracie. As much as she seemed to surround herself with people, she also seemed to be alone much of the time.

He understood loneliness.

He poured himself a cup of coffee and pulled out an order form for a company that supplied the wood he used for the rocking chairs that seemed to be a big hit with locals and curiosity shoppers who were wandering into town. It was a long shot, but maybe he'd keep the store going with rocking chairs and handyman jobs.

It hadn't worked for his family business. But here, where there were no big discount stores, maybe, just maybe, he'd make it. Maybe someday he'd be a local. He liked that idea. He liked the idea of living, not just making a living.

He guessed it had something to do with his dad, losing him to a heart attack in the store he'd given so much of his life to. In the end his dad had been alone, aside from Patrick, because he'd always put the store first.

The front door chimed. He moved through the store, thankful for the distraction of a customer. As he walked he did a quick survey of stocked shelves, stopping to rearrange tools that had gotten moved out of order by an earlier customer.

He smiled at Ann Mars with her topsy-turvy bun and her stooped walk that made her appear even smaller than her barely five feet. She smiled up at him. He loved that she always wore that smile. He didn't doubt for a minute that she'd had her share of hard times but also didn't doubt that smile was genuine.

"Patrick Fogerty, you are a sight for sore eyes."

"Am I really?"

"Of course you are. I have a lightbulb that needs to be replaced and I thought, since you're such a tall drink of water, that you might come over to my shop and replace it for me."

He glanced back at Gracie. She was showing a woman that he knew from church—single, of course—how to brush stain across a cabinet door. The woman glanced his way and then whispered something to Gracie. Gracie smiled a little but she didn't look at him.

Ann Mars cleared her throat.

"Let me tell Gracie where I'm going." He tried not to think about the pile of work in the back room or the stocking he needed to do out front. People first.

A new life and a new outlook.

"You go right ahead. I want to look at these flags you've got in stock."

Gracie glanced his way, her dark eyes shifting from him to her student and then back.

She stepped away from the group of women. "Problem?"

"I'm going to change a lightbulb for Miss Ann. Will you be okay for a few minutes?"

She laughed just a little. "A few minutes? Do you really think you'll get away without visiting her for a little while?"

"I'm going to try. Maybe if I promise to sit down and have coffee with her in a day or two?"

"I'm sure she'd love that." She glanced back at the group. "I think several people would like to have coffee with you."

"Gracie, I'm really not interested." The words came out sharper than he intended and her eyes widened. "I'm sorry."

"Don't worry about it. Go help Miss Ann. I'll be fine here."

The walk to the This 'N' That took less than three minutes. He entered the dark, stuffy interior of Ann Mars's store. A cat ran past him. A cat in the store? He watched it head behind the counter and then heard the telltale sound of scratching in sand.

"Here we go." She pointed to a light above the door that led to the big back room of the store, which was also crowded with used merchandise, shelves, stacks of boxes and who knew what else.

Patrick saw a ladder leaning against a nearby wall. He pulled it out and opened it. As he went up the ladder, Ann held up a bulb.

"Thanks." He grinned down at her.

"You're very welcome. By the way, I heard what you're doing for Merva Duncan and that's real nice of you kids. I wonder, do you think maybe you could do something for Opal Parker?"

Opal. He remembered her from church. An older woman who always wore gloves and a hat to Sunday services. "I think we probably could."

Ann clasped her hands together and smiled. "Oh, that would be wonderful. She's a sweet woman and she tries to keep her place up, but she's getting up in years and it isn't easy for the old gal to get things done."

Old gal? He thought Opal Parker had to be ten years younger than Ann Mars. He swallowed his grin and finished changing the lightbulb. Ann handed up the light fixture and he screwed it into place.

"All done." He started down the ladder.

Ann flipped the switch and the light came on.

"I saw the light," she sang out, then chuckled and smiled up at him. "You are a true gentleman, Patrick. Now, I want to give you some money to help pay for paint. And for flags. I'd like for the folks in town to have flags for their porches."

"Miss Ann, you don't have to."

"I want to. We're all in this together, Patrick."

"I know we are." He tossed the old bulb into the trash.

"I'll bring you a check later." She walked with him to the front door. "Patrick, why isn't a good-looking man like yourself married?"

"I've always been too busy working, Miss Ann."

"Too busy for love? Posh. Who's too busy for love?"

He smiled down at Ann but he wouldn't allow himself to get sucked in, telling her the bits of personal information she and Coraline Connolly seemed to always be digging for. What would he tell them? He'd been busy working, trying to save a family business, and the woman he'd been dating found that a friend of his had more time for her?

His mistake, not hers. He hadn't blamed Geena for wanting someone who could spend time with her.

"I'll see you later, Miss Ann. Let me know if there's anything else I can do for you." He ignored her disappointed look.

"Secrets, Patrick?" She stood on the sidewalk and called out to him. "There's nothing that makes me more curious than a man with secrets."

He waved as he walked back to his store.

* * *

The first Workshop for Women had ended and Gracie felt pretty sure it had been a success. She walked with a few of the women as they made their way out of the store with their new purchases. One of the ladies stopped to admire the rocking chairs that Patrick made.

She watched as her boss headed her way from the This 'N' That. Ann Mars remained on the sidewalk in front of her store, hands on her hips. Gracie smiled and waved at the older woman, who waved back. She doubted the visit had been all about a lightbulb.

She knew the women in this town and how they kept themselves in the middle of everything going on. Patrick was handsome, single and a good Christian. He was a catch.

She wasn't interested in catching another man anytime soon. Her gaze strayed to her boss again. But if a woman *was* going to catch a man, he might as well look like Patrick Fogerty with his broad shoulders and easy smile.

"Introduce me, Gracie." Phyllis Glassner hadn't left. She'd been pretending to look at the plants and now she stood next to Gracie, a bright yellow potted mum in her hands.

"I thought you were dating Johnny Fuller?" Gracie headed for the door. Phyllis followed.

"I was. He's signed up to join the army and said he isn't interested in dating right now, not when he doesn't know where he's going or how long he's going to be gone. And your brother Daniel says he's too busy to date. There isn't much else in this town. Good single men are in as much demand as customers for these stores."

Daniel. Gracie's thoughts rested on her brother. She didn't know what he was up to these days. He worked hard on the farm and at the granary. And then he worked hard on the computer. He said he was taking online classes. She didn't doubt him, but she also didn't know what kind of classes he was taking, and he wasn't telling.

She walked down the aisle of the store to the register. Patrick had entered the store and he straightened a few shelves as he made his way to the back.

Phyllis had followed her to the register with the mum still in her arms. She shot Gracie a pleading look that made her want to groan. Phyllis was the last person she wanted to fix her boss up with. Because… Gracie couldn't think of a good reason. Phyllis was as sweet as she was pretty with her halo of honey-blond hair. She taught Sunday school and raised sheep.

Gracie lifted her gaze again, barely glancing

at Patrick before ducking her head to ring up the mums for Phyllis.

"Anything exciting happen while I was gone?" Patrick walked behind the counter. His arm brushed hers.

Gracie swallowed and looked not at Patrick but at Phyllis.

"No, nothing exciting. Patrick, this is my friend Phyllis."

Patrick held out his hand. "Phyllis, nice to meet you."

"Nice to meet you, too. I wanted to let you know we're having a potluck and movie night next Friday at the church. We'd love to have you join us."

"I might do that." He smiled but then looked down at Gracie. "I need to get an order filled. If you don't need any help up here, I'll be in the back."

She barely had time to respond as he walked away, rounding the counter and heading to the back of the store. Gracie handed Phyllis her change and smiled at the other woman, who wore a disappointed look.

"Well, he's as hard to get to know as they say he is."

"Oh, he really isn't. I think he's just preoccupied. I know he loves brownies, Phyllis."

Phyllis smiled again, her face lighting up and her light gray eyes flashing. "Brownies. Thank you, Gracie!"

Gracie managed a smile. As Phyllis walked away she let out the sigh she'd been holding back. She wasn't a matchmaker. Or the Advice for the Lovelorn columnist.

People shouldn't ask her to help them out in the romance department and she shouldn't be giving anyone advice. She'd royally messed up her own life.

She rested her elbows on the counter and covered her face with her hands. One of these days people would stop asking why she'd walked out on the most eligible bachelor in the county. People would stop gossiping.

In a small town, there would be another scandal. Someday.

A hand touched her shoulder. She jumped a little and looked up. Patrick handed her a glass of iced tea.

"You okay?"

She nodded and sipped the tea. "Yeah, I'm good."

"You don't look good." He grinned and shook his head. "That didn't come out right. You look great. Beautiful as… You know what I mean."

"I do. And I have a mirror. I know how bad I look."

"Do you need to take a day off?"

"No, I want to take off. Maybe to a deserted island, one without my dad and brothers. One without the *Bygones Gazette* and hundreds of people who think they know the scoop about their own local Runaway Bride." She frowned. "Is that too much information?"

"Not at all. I think we all have days like that. Your last couple of weeks have been one extreme to another."

"True. I was going to be married, and now I'm back at home with my dad and my brothers. And my brothers are a mess. They're either trying to fix things for me, or they're asking me to fix something for them. They're helpless and I made them that way."

"I think they're all old enough to take care of themselves."

"Yes, they are, aren't they?" She looked at the *Gazette* that she'd been reading through that morning before the store opened. "And maybe it's about time I let them take care of themselves?"

"You aren't going to leave Bygones, are you? Because I'm not sure I can survive this town without your help."

"You have Coraline and Ann."

"Very true, but they can't sand cabinets, build bookcases or show a customer how to install a ceiling fan." He had remained next to her, towering over her in his flannel shirt, close enough for her to detect the scent of pine and citrus. "And the other problem with Coraline and Ann is that they can't imagine a guy being single and happy."

Gracie slid the paper in front of her, ignoring his happily-single comment that would crush the hearts of so many single women in Bygones. "I'm not leaving Bygones. I guess I'll never leave."

"You know, marriage isn't the only way to leave town."

"You're right." She looked over the paper again. "But I don't want to leave. I think it is time I get my own place."

A place of her own. She had thought about it a lot over the past week. A place she decorated herself with food she picked for herself. She could eat frozen dinners every night if she wanted. She could date without her brothers standing guard, questioning anyone who came to pick her up.

The front door chimed and Ann Mars made

her way through the store for the second time that day. She looked at the two of them, her eyes narrowing as she studied them.

"Patrick. Gracie. I thought you had a store full of customers."

"It's the afternoon lull," Patrick explained as he walked out from behind the counter. "Do you need something else, Miss Ann?"

"No, not at all. I was just bored and thought I'd make my rounds and bring you that check. What's that serious look for, Gracie?"

Gracie looked up from the paper and managed a half smile for the older woman. "I'm thinking about getting a place of my own."

"Well, I think that's a wonderful idea. Do you have a place in mind?"

"No, I was just going to look through the *Gazette*. But there isn't much in here."

"The most interesting thing in that issue of the *Gazette* is the story of the Bygones Runaway Bride." Ann cackled and her thin, gray brows arched. "Oh, that's you, isn't it?"

"I guess it is."

"Well, honey, it just so happens I have a little one-bedroom house for rent."

Gracie perked up, her smile widening. "Really? Is it expensive?"

"Can you mow a lawn, maybe help an old gal clean her house and do some other odd jobs?"

"Of course I can."

"Then it's yours for utilities. If you can just help out my sister Lottie, you've got a house."

"Oh, Ann, thank you." Gracie left her place behind the counter to hug the woman that even she towered over.

"You're welcome, Gracie. I'm glad I finally found someone I can trust. Lottie isn't as well as she used to be and she needs a little help from time to time."

"When can I move in?"

"This weekend should be fine. It's furnished. You'll just need a few dishes and blankets."

Gracie had a place of her own. She would be twenty-five in a month and she was finally going to live in her own place. For a girl who had lived at home even while attending a nearby community college, this was a big deal.

Ann Mars glanced out the window. "Well, what do you know, I have customers. I guess I'll hurry on back to my store. Gracie, come by later and I'll get your key."

"Thank you again, Miss Ann."

"You're welcome, Gracie." Ann Mars waved as she started toward the door. "Patrick, you owe me a cup of coffee."

"Yes, ma'am."

Gracie smiled at her boss and then watched as the older woman hurried, at her own hurrying pace, out of the store and down the sidewalk. There were a few cars on Main Street. Gracie walked to the door and looked out, watching as several people hurried into the Cozy Cup Café. A woman walked out of the Fluff & Stuff carrying a little dog and a bag of merchandise. As she watched, an older gentleman stopped to sit in one of Patrick's chairs.

"Sometimes I think the town is going to survive." She glanced back at Patrick. He walked through the store and joined her at the window.

"I hope so. I know I'm not a local, but I'm pretty invested in the survival of this town, too."

"I would hate it if you…" She bit down on her lip and focused on the older man in the rocking chair. "It would be a shame to lose you and this store. And if the town makes it, we'll be able to rehire the men the police force laid off. Not to mention the men my dad had to let go. My brothers aren't all about running the granary."

"It's hard taking over a family business." Patrick stood next to her, a giant of a man with a quiet voice. "I have to admit I had times when I resented our family business. It took a lot of my dad's time. And then it took a lot of mine."

"Is that why you've never been married?" Gracie regretted the question the minute it left her lips. "I'm sorry, that's none of my business."

He smiled down at her. "How about dinner, Gracie? I've got a great loaf of bread upstairs, some lunch meat that doesn't smell sour and a bag of chips that haven't gone stale."

"That sounds wonderful…I think."

A car door slammed. A minute later, Trent Morgan walked into the hardware store.

Patrick stood between her and Trent, unrelenting, as if he didn't plan on letting her ex-fiancé pass by. Gracie slipped out from behind him. She knew how to take care of herself. And she definitely didn't need another man in her life thinking he had to protect her.

She had her dad and five brothers for that. She was always amazed how they could be so overprotective and so needy, all at the same time.

"Trent." She bit down on her bottom lip and waited. She was aware of Patrick moving away.

"I'll be in the back," he informed them as he left. She smiled at the space he was giving her, but also the tone of his voice. He was here if she needed him.

Trent watched Patrick go and then turned his attention back to her. Gracie wished she was taller. Even a few inches would have given her a more level playing field. She wanted to stand on tiptoes and stare him down, let him know she couldn't be intimidated. Much.

He looked around the store. "I would like to know why you embarrassed us all the way you did. And I'd like to know what you plan to do about the money my family spent on our wedding."

"I'd like to know how long you were dating your secretary and if you would have stopped after we were married."

"We had that discussion, and I told you, she's someone I've known a long time. I'm not giving up old friends because I'm getting married."

"You're not getting married, so now you can see her whenever you want." Gracie shot a quick look toward the back of the store. She didn't want everyone in Bygones to know her humiliation. She didn't want Patrick to know.

"You knew about her weeks before the wedding."

"I wanted to trust you. You proved I couldn't."

He let out a long sigh. "Fine."

"So let your mom know that you can pay for the wedding because you're the one who decided to cheat." There, she'd done it. She faced him, unwilling to bow down.

He shook his head and walked out the door.

Gracie covered her face with her hands and breathed in, breathed past the pain of disillusionment and regret. The door chimed and she pulled her hands from her face to see Whitney Leigh heading her way.

Gracie brushed a hand through her hair, drew in a breath and faced the reporter for the *Gazette*.

"Whitney, now isn't a good time."

Whitney held up both hands and smiled. "I know it isn't. That's why I'm not here on official business. I was down the street getting a cup of coffee."

"I wish you would have brought me a cup."

"Are you okay?" Whitney looked around the store, as if the conversation was a little out of her comfort zone. Whitney, who didn't mind quizzing people to get a good interview, a good story, was trying to be…a friend.

"I'm good."

"If you need to talk, I'm here."

Gracie smiled. "Off the record?"

"Yes, off the record. I'm sorry about the Bygones Runaway Bride article, but really, the paper sold more copies last week than ever before."

"I'm a hit."

"You're definitely a hit. And probably lucky to have escaped Trent Morgan."

"And his mother." She laughed a little and wiped at the few tears that clung to her lashes.

"That's what I like about you, Gracie Wilson. You always look on the bright side."

"I try."

A customer walked through the door, gave them both a curious look and headed for the paint section.

"I should go, but call if you need anything." Whitney waved as she left.

Gracie started in the direction of the customer but Patrick was already helping him. He smiled at her and winked. Her heart, still recovering from the encounter with Trent, quaked a little. Maybe in fear for its safety.

Patrick had invited her to have dinner with him. No, not really dinner. A hopefully not-spoiled lunch-meat sandwich. Now, watching him, she questioned if the invitation had been serious. Maybe she should let him off the hook. At closing time she could get her purse and keys and leave. Or she could make an excuse.

Or she could stay and have dinner with a nice guy. No strings attached. Because she was single. She was having a difficult time coming to terms with that reality. She no longer had a ring on her finger or Trent's picture on her key chain.

She didn't have a home of her own or a husband to call when something went wrong.

She was really and truly single.

Chapter Seven

Patrick locked up the register at the end of the day and watched as Gracie turned the sign to Closed. He wanted to protect her. He had told himself earlier, during the moment when he wanted to run Trent Morgan out of the store, that he wanted to protect her because she looked like a woman who needed to be protected. She was young. She looked frail, although he knew that she wasn't.

She was as tough as nails.

Whatever had happened between her and Trent was her business.

She walked back to the counter and picked up the bag from the bakery that still contained a few pastries. When she looked up at him, there was a softness in her dark eyes. Yeah, he guessed she was tough, but she was also vulnerable.

"I should go." She straightened, the bag held close like a shield.

"Where are you going?"

"Home."

"I thought we were having sandwiches. And then we could run over to your new house to see if you need anything."

She opened the bag and peeked in at the contents. She finally looked up, smiling just a little. "I don't know."

"You have something against slightly sour lunch meat?"

She laughed, the sound light and easy. He had to be losing his mind, because he wanted to kiss her, and that was the biggest mistake he could make. She worked for him. She'd just walked away from a wedding and, for whatever reason, the jilted groom was coming around again.

Kissing her could make things more complicated than he wanted them to be.

And yet, he'd offered her supper. As simple as sandwiches were, they still meant a meal together.

"Okay." She sighed as she agreed to his offer.

"You sound thrilled. I could probably heat up a frozen pizza if sandwiches are the problem."

"I really don't want food poisoning. If we both

get sick, who will run the store? Worse, everyone will know that we ate together."

"Scary."

They walked through the back door to the steps that led to his apartment. Rufus the dog trotted down the alley in their direction and followed them up the stairs. Gracie walked with her head down, distracted.

He let her remain in her private thoughts; everyone had them. When they walked through the door of his loft apartment, she looked up and smiled again.

"I love this place."

"It's growing on me. When I first moved to Bygones, I thought I'd have a house, maybe some land and a few head of cattle."

"You want to be a farmer?"

He flipped on overhead lights as they walked into the kitchen. "I think not a farmer, but I definitely want space."

"I don't think I would have loved living in Manhattan. I wanted the house, the dream…"

"You know, it could still work out."

"No, it can't." She settled herself on a chair, and Rufus, who had managed to squeeze in the door with them, sat at her feet. "What can I do to help?"

"I've got it covered. You can sit there and keep me company."

"Right."

He opened the freezer and took out a frozen pizza. When he turned back around she was in the kitchen, opening cabinets. She pulled out a couple of glasses.

"Gracie, when was the last time you sat and didn't help?"

She shrugged off the question as she held the glasses under the ice maker in the fridge door. "I don't know. I'm just filling glasses with ice."

"Go sit down. Take a break."

She set the cups on the counter, ran her hand along the granite top and returned, slowly, to her chair. He smiled as he filled the glasses with iced tea and handed her one.

"Thank you." She lifted the glass and took a sip.

"What will your dad and brothers do without you?" He shouldn't have asked, but the question came out. He looked at the pizza box and turned on the oven to the correct temperature.

"I guess they'll eat out a lot. And probably call me every time they can't find something. Or when something needs to be washed. They're pretty helpless." She ran a finger down the outside of the glass, wiping away the condensation. "I guess I've done too much for them."

"They'll survive. They're all grown men, Gracie. You deserve to have your own place. They would have been alone, anyway."

"If I'd gone through with the wedding. Yes, I've thought about that." She nodded in agreement. "Do you want me to make a salad or something?"

"No, I've got it. And you wouldn't want a salad made from the lettuce in my fridge. It's a little beyond green and crispy."

She shuddered and grimaced. "Do you need me to go to the store for you?"

She was leaning on the bar, her chin resting on her hands, her elbows on the countertop. She was completely serious about going to the store for him. The moment and her offer took him by surprise and he laughed.

And then he leaned in, placed his hands on her cheeks and kissed her. He meant it to be a light and easy gesture that fit the moment.

The moment changed.

His lips lingered on hers and she leaned toward him, the counter between them. He wanted it gone. He wanted nothing between them. But he guessed there was more than the counter keeping them apart.

Her lips on his made him push aside misgivings. He kissed her tenderly and then broke away long enough to move around the counter to her side. He waited a brief moment, waiting for her to tell him they couldn't do this. Instead she moved her hands to his shoulders. He touched her cheek and leaned in, settling into the kiss that he'd thought to end.

Her fingers moved down his arms as he continued in an incredible moment that he didn't want to end. He was a grown man and his world had just been rocked by the woman whose soft, dark hair slipped between his fingers, whose lips stilled beneath his.

He pulled back, took a deep breath and waited for words to form. Gracie's lips were parted and her fingers lingered there, her eyes wide as she looked at him.

"I'm sorry." He shook his head, because he didn't want to sound sorry. "That's wrong. I'm not sorry. But I'm not sure what else to say. Gracie, I'm not sure what to think."

"Me, neither, but thank you." She smiled a little and her hand held his. "I think I've been numb for a long time, and this gives me hope. Not that I'm looking to move on. Or find someone to replace Trent."

"I'm glad I could be of some assistance." He

rubbed the back of his neck as he looked at the woman sitting across from him. The dog moved between them, looking up with questioning eyes. Patrick gave him a look. "What?"

The timer on the stove went off. Patrick grabbed an oven mitt off the counter and walked back to the stove. He leaned to pull the pizza from the oven. Gracie giggled and he glanced up. He set the pizza on the top of the stove and waited.

"I'm sorry." She wiped at her eyes. "It's just, the kitty oven mitt, and you, big, tall you."

She laughed again and the sound was contagious. He chuckled as he pulled off the mitt with pictures of kittens.

"My mom gave it to me as a housewarming gift."

"I like it." She leaned her chin on her folded hands, elbows propped on the countertop. His eyes strayed to the lips he'd recently kissed. He had to shake loose and focus.

"Thank you. The joke is that I don't like cats."

"You don't like cats! Who doesn't like cats?"

"Lots of people?" He cut the pizza and used a spatula to slide a couple of slices onto a plate. He set it on the counter in front of her.

"I don't know. I think most people love cats. Miss Ann loves cats."

"I saw one in her store today."

"I'll let you off the hook. I'm not fond of cats. I'm allergic and when I was a kid we had a cat that scratched my face." She pointed to her cheek and he noticed, for the first time, a faint scar.

"So, we have something in common." He carried his plate around to sit next to her. They were talking about cats. They'd just kissed and she'd thanked him for that. Now the conversation had turned to cats. He shook his head as he reached for Parmesan cheese.

"We have a lot in common. We both love Bygones. We both want the stores and the town to survive." She took the cheese from him and he wondered why the list of likes.

"That we do. And we'd both like to know who funded all this money."

"Do you think it was Mr. Randall?" She took a bite of her pizza and chewed thoughtfully as he considered an answer. He had several thoughts on who it might be and wasn't sure how much he wanted to say.

"It might be. I'm not sure."

"But you have to have a clue who gave you money. Who do you pay back if you leave before the two years are up?"

"I'm not sure."

"Doesn't that worry you? That you moved here and put all this time into something, hoping to make it in a town you've never been to, and you have no idea who is funding this venture?"

"A little. But I prayed about it, Gracie. I knew I had to leave Michigan. I knew I needed a fresh start and this door opened."

"Why did you need a fresh start? Most people want a fresh start when something goes wrong." She smiled up at him, her expression soft, her eyes luminous. "Case in point. Me."

"Why do you ask so many questions?"

"You're in the witness-protection program." Her eyes widened and she smiled, then laughed. "This is some elaborate government plan to hide government witnesses!"

"That's it. I can't believe you guessed."

"I'm very smart." She wiped her hands on a napkin. "And I'm ready to go see my new house."

Her phone rang and she reached into her purse, which hung on the back of her bar stool. The smile she'd worn disappeared.

"Hi, Dad." Gracie walked away from Patrick. The apartment was open, with the dining room and kitchen connected to the living room. Floor-to-ceiling windows looked out over Main Street.

"Gracie, I got a message on my phone that you wouldn't be home until later. Is everything okay?"

She leaned against the cool glass of the window, watching as Ann Mars walked out of her store and down the street, a cat following behind her. Midway down the street Ann turned, as if she sensed she was being watched. She looked up and around. Gracie moved back from the window. What she and Patrick didn't need were rumors about their relationship.

"Gracie?"

"I'm here. Dad, I'm going to look at a house Ann Mars has offered me."

"A house? What in the world do you need a house for?"

"Well, I'm almost twenty-five and I think I should try living on my own. When I think about what I almost did, going from living with my dad to living with Trent, it scares me a little. I think I need to do this, to find out who I am."

A long pause followed. She heard her dad take a deep breath on the other end of the line.

"Gracie, you know I'll miss you around here, but you're right. You should do this. I think you've stayed home thinking you need to take care of us guys. But we can do a lot more for ourselves than you think."

"I know you can," she said, and they both laughed.

"And I guess you'd like to live your life not always having your dad or an older brother as a guardian."

"It would be nice. And, Dad, it isn't like I'm moving out of state or even to another town. I'll be right here."

"I know you will. So, when does the big move take place?"

"This weekend." Two weeks after her failed attempt at getting married, she was moving out. She closed her eyes and thought about how life changed in a matter of moments.

She thought that God probably hadn't been surprised by any of this. She was surprised by a lot of things, like kissing Patrick.

"You'll need furniture." Her dad broke into her thoughts.

"It's furnished."

"I guess you're good to go, then."

She guessed she was. She told him she loved him and ended the call. But she had almost told him she wouldn't do it, that she wouldn't move.

"Everything okay?"

She turned away from the window. "Other than I think Ann Mars might have seen me up here, and I'm worried my dad and brothers won't survive without me?"

"I think those are all problems you can handle. Gracie, I think you can handle just about anything."

She smiled at that. She'd always been a strange combination of independent but over-protected. That happened to a girl in a family of men. She knew she could handle what life threw at her. She always had. But alone? As much as it scared her, she looked forward to it.

"Let's go look at that house." He grabbed his keys off the counter. "Ready?"

"I am."

A few minutes later they were pulling up to the little house behind Ann's sister Lottie's place. The house might have been a detached garage at one time. Now it was a one-bedroom cottage with vines creeping up the sides and flower beds growing out of control.

For a minute they sat in Patrick's extended-cab truck. Gracie glanced at her boss. He reached for his door handle.

"It looks solid," he offered.

"It looks perfect. Let's go check it out."

With Patrick at her side, Gracie unlocked the front door of the cottage and entered her new home. Her new life. The house was tiny—a miniature living room, miniature kitchen and bedroom with a bathroom attached. The floors were linoleum with big flowers, circa 1950. The kitchen had white painted cabinets with yellow Formica tops. A window overlooked a vegetable garden that had gone to weeds and several bird feeders that needed filling.

Gracie wandered through the house, from the bedroom with the blond-stained wood furniture back to the living room with the dark green sofa and recliner. A few area rugs, some pictures on the walls and she could see this as her home. She tried not to think about the house she would have shared with Trent. It would have been too big, that French country brick house. It would have been another world.

This was her world. Her life. She smiled and spun around to face Patrick. He was poking around at a water spot on the ceiling.

"I love it." She grinned and hoped he'd smile and not say something negative. Her dad and brothers always used negativity to bring her down and make her see reality. Their version of reality.

The car she'd wanted when she turned sixteen would have been a gas guzzler. The basketball player who had asked her out, he was from another town and she didn't know a thing about him. When she'd wanted to go away to college, they'd convinced her to make the drive and save money.

And they were usually right. But sometimes, just every now and then, she wanted to find out for herself.

They had tried to warn her about Trent. Evan had been blunt about what he thought of her future intended.

"I think you're right." Patrick lowered his hand. "I can fix that. It probably needs a seam in the roof sealed a little better."

"Thank you." She reached for his hand and gave it a squeeze. "But I can fix it, too."

The screen door creaked open. Ann Mars stepped into the room. She surveyed the two of them and then turned her attention to the house. She looked around, nodding as if she approved.

"I thought it might be the two of you." She flicked a speck of lint off the sofa. "My sister is a worrier and she called me to let me know we had trespassers."

"I should have let her know we were coming back to look at the house." Gracie let go of Patrick's hand. She hadn't been paying attention until Ann glanced down at their joined hands.

"It isn't a problem, Gracie. I only wanted to

know that it would work for you. What do you think? Is it furnished okay?"

"It's perfect." Gracie glanced around the little house. "Oh, Patrick noticed a water leak."

"I can fix it, though," he offered.

"That would be so nice. And if it is going to be expensive, you let me know. Lottie lives the life of a miser, but she and her husband made some good investments over the years. She can afford to keep this place maintained."

"Thanks, Ann." Gracie turned to take one last walk through her new home. She flipped off lights that she'd left on and rejoined Patrick and Miss Ann Mars in the living room.

"It's perfect. And you let me know what I need to do for Lottie."

Ann cackled at that. "Oh, don't worry, Lottie will let you know. And a word of warning, she's nosier than I am and she'll be watching like a hawk. She also isn't as good at keeping things to herself."

"Ann, what you—"

Ann cut Gracie off with a raised hand, her gnarled fingers shaking a little. "Don't try to fool an old lady, Gracie. I am very aware and my eyes are quite good."

"I'm sure they are." She rubbed at her cheeks as heat climbed from her neck into her face.

"Oh, Gracie, don't look so shocked. You're a grown woman and Patrick is a grown, single man." Ann looped an arm through Patrick's and led them outside. "I think the two of you look rather sweet together. Big, tall Patrick and sweet little Gracie."

"Ann, you're mistaken." Patrick glanced at Gracie and then at Ann Mars. His dark cheeks were tinged with red. "Gracie and I are friends."

"That's the best way to start a relationship, Patrick, as friends. Some couples fall into love but never get to know each other. It's a shame, really. They miss out on so much."

"Ann, we're really not a couple. I just ended an engagement less than two weeks ago." Even as she said the words, Gracie knew that Ann wasn't hearing. She'd already made up her mind.

"And aren't you glad you did?" Ann took careful steps toward Lottie's house, still holding Patrick's arm. "I'm not sure why you stood that young man up at the altar, and I don't care what other people say, but I know you, Gracie, and I know you had a good reason. It wasn't just a case of cold feet."

Gracie didn't know what to say. Patrick glanced over at her, a look Ann Mars didn't see but must have felt because she looked up at him. He smiled down at her, a perfectly innocent smile, Gracie thought. A smile that could make a woman forget that she'd recently had her heart broken.

It took her by surprise. And not much surprised Gracie.

Chapter Eight

Thursday evening Patrick couldn't come up with a decent excuse to get out of the social night at the Community Church. Everyone was going to be there, Coraline Connolly had informed him, and he was part of everyone. He had walked the short distance to the church that already felt like home to him.

Yes, there were still a few locals who weren't thrilled with the changes to Main Street. That was how small towns operated, Joshua Smith had told him. And Josh was at this function, along with Lily Farnsworth and Tate Bronson. The two were happily engaged and planning a wedding to take place pretty soon.

He hadn't seen Melissa Sweeney and her fiancé, Brian, but he'd seen the cake on display in the fellowship hall and knew she must have brought it from her shop, Sweet Dreams Bakery.

Allison True, owner of the new bookstore, was also in attendance and she stood with a group of Bygones's longtime citizens.

Allison was the only shop owner in the group who was originally from Bygones. It made sense that she knew people, that she had connections and friendships with the citizens of the town.

He searched the crowd for Gracie, not really expecting to find her. But he wanted her to be there. He wanted to stand next to her, the two of them facing these crowds of people. Together. He shook off the thoughts. When had he ever needed someone standing next to him? And Gracie? Five-feet-tall Gracie?

Made-of-steel Gracie. He smiled; it fit her.

A hand grabbed his arm and pulled him to a stop as he started through the crowd. He turned and smiled at the woman whose hold on his arm kept him from escaping. Phyllis. He couldn't remember her last name but she'd been in the store the other day and had invited him to this function. He had a sneaking suspicion that she thought his appearance equaled a date.

He glanced around, wondering again where Gracie was and why she wasn't here.

"Patrick, I'm so glad you're here!" She was pretty, and he was sure she was sweet.

"I was just heading into the fellowship hall to speak to Coraline Connolly."

"Oh, of course." Her smile faded. "Maybe we can chat later. I think we plan on eating in about thirty minutes. And after that they're showing a movie."

"Great. I'll talk to you soon." He was a chicken. He was bad at relationships. He didn't like the singles scene. Back in Michigan his friends had all gotten married, were having kids and insisting that he be the next to fall. He'd been set up on more blind dates than he cared to remember.

Most had been torture. Some had been nice. A few of the women he'd gone out with more than once. But work had always interfered.

A friend of his had accused him of letting work sabotage his love life. He'd told Patrick that when the right woman came along, he'd ignore the phone, the million odd jobs he tended to take on, and he'd learn to take a day or two off.

"Patrick, there you are." Coraline Connolly headed his way, her short hair neat as always, her business attire never changing. He'd seen her once in jeans and a blouse, but almost always in a skirt and jacket that screamed school principal.

"Here I am." And already looking for an escape. "Have you seen Gracie?"

Coraline glanced around the room. "No, I haven't. That girl is hiding out in the little house Ann let her move into. And I doubt she's going to come to a function that focuses on socializing and singles. I think she's had her share of romance for a while."

"Yes, she probably has."

"Is there a reason you were looking for her?" Coraline's eyes sparked with interest.

"I needed to see if she could open for me tomorrow. I have a job at the Scott ranch, fixing a bathroom floor. And then I have to take a look at a couple of the houses we're going to paint."

"About that painting. Patrick, I am so thrilled with that idea. I'm sure Gracie dragged you along on one of her little schemes, but it's brilliant."

"She does have a tendency to pull a person into her plans."

"Yes, well, she's always managed to get so much done. I think we would have missed her if she'd married Trent Morgan. Even engaged to him she was losing a little of herself. It's good to see her returning to the person we all know and love."

"I would have hated to lose her, too."

Coraline's eyes widened and she coughed a little. He realized his mistake.

"I worded that wrong," he rushed to explain. "I meant, I would have hated to lose her at the hardware store. The Fixer-Upper needs her. She knows how to bring in customers."

"She went to school to get a degree in marketing." Coraline looked away, smiled a little and then looked back at him.

Patrick glanced the way she'd looked, wondering who had gotten that secret smile of hers. He saw a group of people near the food but no one stood out. Interesting.

And on to other interesting news that had taken him by surprise. "Gracie has a degree in marketing?"

Coraline shook her head. "No, unfortunately she didn't finish. She went for three years but the expense of going, and the exhaustion from school, the farm and the granary, it all got to be too much for her. She's never slowed down to let people take care of her."

"I can see that."

"And I can see you have other things on your mind, Patrick. If you need to talk, you know that I'm here. And if you're worried about the store, don't be. I know you're going to make it here in Bygones."

"Thanks, Coraline, I appreciate the vote of confidence."

She patted his arm and walked away. And that left him in the open again. From across the room, Phyllis waved. He nodded in answer and smiled. Another group of women seemed to be in earnest communication. A few of them glanced his way. One started to break from the group.

He had to get out of here.

He pulled out his phone and dialed a familiar number. When Gracie answered, he felt something like relief sweep over him. He walked away from the crowds of people, relaxing as he went.

"Hello," she repeated.

"Where are you?" he finally asked, sounding a lot more perturbed than he'd planned.

"Wow, you sound pleasant." She huffed and puffed as they talked. "Where are you?"

"I'm at a church function surrounded by single women. I thought you'd be here to support me."

"You don't need me for a wingman."

He laughed at that. "No, I don't. I thought you'd be here, though."

"As a shield of protection?"

"Yes, I guess so." He kept talking as he headed for the back door, ignoring the people who sent curious looks his way. He guessed the newcomers to town did more than bring revenue; they gave the locals something new to talk about.

"Sorry, I'm busy trying to peel decades-old wallpaper off the kitchen walls."

"Why would you do that?"

"Because I want to paint before I move in. I'm not fond of big red-and-blue flowers. I mean, not that I'm against flowers, or even against red and blue, but last night I had a dream that flowers were trying to chase me down and strangle me."

His tension completely gone, he laughed. "Why not put up tile? We could scrape the wallpaper to rough it up and you wouldn't have to peel it."

"Now you tell me."

"I have some natural tile, different-size squares. It would look great."

"So I just have to peel paint from the big wall where my table is."

"I guess so." He pulled his keys out of his pocket as he walked across the parking lot to his truck. "What do you have for dinner?"

"Huh?"

"I'll stop at the store and get the tile and other supplies. I'll be at your place in thirty minutes."

He was losing his mind. He could think of no other reason for what he'd just done, walking out of a church full of singles and then hightailing it to Gracie Wilson's. He'd escaped the frying pan and jumped right into the fire.

Gracie looked at the phone in her hand and then she grabbed the stainless toaster and glared at her reflection in the polished metal of the antique kitchen appliance. Eek. Not good. She had flecks of paint on her face and in her hair from the bathroom project she had already finished. She tossed her phone on the counter and looked again at the scraggly ponytail with hair escaping from all sides.

Her hunky, adorable and single boss was going to catch her looking like a wreck. Not that she wanted to impress him. After all, he'd seen her with a puffy, tear-stained face. He'd seen, firsthand, the humiliation of what happened to a hometown girl when she left the guy at the altar.

Okay, she didn't want to impress him, but she didn't want to get caught looking like a home-repair project, either. She rushed into the bedroom and grabbed a pair of jeans and a clean T-shirt. Heart racing, she did a quick change, scrubbed paint off her face and ran a brush through her hair. She glanced at lip gloss but she refused to go that far. He would know she was up to something if he knocked on her door and found her wearing makeup that she almost never wore.

The lip gloss tempted her again. The bright pink gloss smelled like apples. She gave in to temptation and brushed it across her lips. And then she fell further and sprayed a quick squirt of perfume.

And then regret hit. She looked like someone who had gotten ready for a guy. And she was the last person who should be doing something so ridiculous. She'd just walked away from something that had been more than just a relationship. She had been moments away from marriage.

That was obviously over, but she didn't want to start a new relationship, not now when she still doubted herself and wondered if Trent had been right, that she was the reason he'd cheated.

But friendship. Patrick was about the best friend she had right now.

A knock on the door brought her eyes open. She glanced quickly in the mirror and then hurried to the living room, sliding on the linoleum as she crossed the room. Patrick stood on the other side of the storm door, holding a brown paper bag and smiling.

She motioned him inside. "What's that?"

"Burgers and fries."

Her stomach growled. They both laughed.

"Come on in. Sorry that everything is a mess. Including me. I painted the bathroom today and then I started in on that horrible wallpaper."

"The stuff nightmares are made of."

She motioned to the little dining-room table with the aluminum frame and yellow Formica circa 1960-something. The chairs matched but they were covered with avocado-green vinyl, probably compliments of the early 1970s. Somehow it all worked and she loved it.

"Have a seat. Do you want water or iced tea?"

He folded himself into the chair, looking like a giant trying to sit on a toy. "Water is good."

"So, you didn't enjoy the social at the Community Church?"

"It wasn't terrible, just not my favorite thing to do."

"You'd rather spackle some plaster on the wall and put up tile? That's a little weird."

He shrugged powerful shoulders beneath a denim shirt. "I guess it is."

She filled glasses with water and grabbed a couple of paper plates for their dinner. When she returned to the table, he stood and then there was that awkward moment when chivalry takes a girl by surprise. Gracie stared up at him, unsure of what to say next. Her heart was beating fast as she opened the bag of food and placed a burger and fries on each of their plates.

He plucked at her hair and she was forced to look up again, forced to see his smile and laughter in his eyes.

"You have paint in your hair." He slid his fingers down a strand and flicked the paint away. "There, got it. Or some of it."

Heat climbed her cheeks and she sat down quickly, barely hitting the edge of the seat, but fortunately not adding to her embarrassment by falling on the floor. Patrick's hand shot out and he steadied her.

"I'm a klutz." She unwrapped her burger.

Patrick's hand reached for hers, his fingers closing over hers with a strong but tender touch. "I'll pray."

"Please do." She didn't mean to make it sound as if she needed prayer. "For the food. I mean for the food."

He leaned close and prayed, "Amen. And, Gracie, calm down."

She looked up, swallowing the lump that had formed in her throat. "I'm trying."

"I'm sorry about the kiss. I know I shouldn't have."

"It's really okay." But he was right. She couldn't stop thinking about the kiss. It had happened and now they had to move on and find their way back to who they really were. He was her boss. She needed her job and couldn't let that one kiss come between them.

"No, it isn't. You work for me. I shouldn't have crossed that line."

"I let you cross the line." She smiled as she said it, hoping to ease the tension. It was a strange tension, lingering between them like a wire pulled tight and then flicked to make it buzz.

A guitar string. Her thoughts did a strange rambling thing when she was nervous, going in all directions but where they needed to go.

Patrick's big hand still held hers. He lifted it and kissed her knuckles. "It's okay."

Yeah, it was okay, unless he kept doing overly sweet things like kissing her hand, like bringing her dinner and looking at her the way he did. Because he made her feel as if she was perfect the way she was, even in old jeans and a T-shirt with paint in her hair.

"I know. I know that I made the right decision." She looked up, a French fry in her hand. "Why haven't you ever been married? You'd make a great husband."

"Is that a proposal?"

They both laughed. "No, I think I'm probably not ready for a proposal. But I wonder, because usually women say that all the good men are taken. And you're one of the good ones, but you're not taken."

He sighed, exhaling slowly, and she knew she'd just dug past the surface of Patrick Fogerty. He let her hand go, placing it gently on the table.

"Gracie, my name is Patrick Fogerty and I'm a workaholic." He smiled as he said it but Gracie saw the pain in his eyes and knew it wasn't a joke. "I know that sounds a little dramatic, but that's who I am and one of the reasons I came here. Being a workaholic can be as damaging to a person as any other addiction, I guess. It's bad for your health. It's pretty hard on relationships. People you love suffer from neglect."

"Patrick, I'm sorry."

"No, don't be. It isn't as if I don't know some of your secrets. I did find you in your wedding dress."

"Very true. I guess that alone entitles me to at least one of your secrets."

"Okay, I was the one jilted. I dated a woman named Geena. And Geena married my best friend. I think because she saw him more than she saw me."

"I'm really sorry."

"Don't be. She deserved a lot better than I gave her."

He stood up, tossed the wrappers and paper plate into the trash and smiled down at her. She craned her head to look up at him. "And I'm getting a lot better at slowing down and making time for people."

"Sometimes the hard things happen so that God can bring the good things."

He continued to watch her and she got up, needing to avoid that look and the feelings that accompanied it. She tossed her papers into the trash and rinsed her hands off at the sink.

"I think that's probably true." He stood, moving to the middle of the kitchen and looking around. "I'm in Bygones because I saw myself becoming my dad."

Gracie waited but he didn't give her more than that and she wasn't going to push.

"I say we get started." Patrick headed for the front door. "I have the supplies in the truck."

"Let me get shoes."

"I can get the supplies. I'll be right back."

Gracie watched him walk across the yard to his truck. She had five minutes to get her act together, to stop seeing him as a man who needed to be fixed. To stop seeing him as a man who could heal her very damaged heart.

Chapter Nine

"One more section." Patrick watched as Gracie measured the tiles and arranged them. He smiled down at her because she wasn't watching, so intent was she on her project. Her mouth was pressed in a firm line, her bottom lip between her teeth. "You should take a deep breath and roll your shoulders to relax."

She looked up, her dark eyes focusing on his face. He bent his legs and squatted next to her. "Gracie, relax."

"I'm relaxed. I'm just concentrating."

"You look as wound up as an eight-day clock."

She laughed a little and took his advice, rolling her shoulders and then moving her head from side to side to relieve the kinks that had to be tightening her neck muscles.

"There, better?" she asked as she once again bent her head over her project.

"Oh, sure, of course." He reached for her hand. "Come on, you've got it all done. Let's put those tiles up."

He stood and brought her to her feet with him. She leaned again to pick up the squares of tile, placing them on the counter in the order they should go on the wall.

"So, the first house we'll paint starting Tuesday evening?" She handed him the squares and he put them on the wall, adjusting them only slightly from her original design.

"Yes." He looked down at her as he placed another tile. "And we've got quite a bit of help. Whitney Leigh is a great one to get involved because she knows how to get people signed up."

"She is good at that."

"You're still upset over the article about your wedding."

She shrugged slim shoulders. "Not really. I do like Whitney. I haven't enjoyed everyone in town discussing my life like it was, um, yesterday's news."

She smiled at him but he could see that it still hurt.

"Gracie, the other day when Trent was at the store... Are the two of you trying to work things out?"

She shook her head. "No, not at all."

But he had to wonder if she *wanted* to work

things out. She'd never revealed why the wedding was called off. He didn't see her as a flighty woman who suddenly changed her mind for no reason. Even cold feet, his early assumption, didn't seem to fit.

"There, all done." He placed the last square and they stood back, side by side, looking at a job well done. "I can help you paint. Sunday after church if that works for you."

"You don't have to. Really, I can do it."

"I know you can do it." He also knew when to back off. He walked over to the sink and washed his hands. When he turned, she was picking up the odds and ends they'd left scattered around the kitchen. She had a box and she filled it with tools, leftover tiles and other supplies he'd dragged in.

"I really owe you for this." She finished cleaning up and joined him at the sink to wash her hands. "And it's so much cozier than just painting the walls. I love it."

"Good, then it was worth it. And you saved me from an evening of endless matchmaking." He dried his hands and handed her the towel. "Part of which you were responsible for."

She turned a little bit pink. "Sorry about that. But really, there are some nice women in Bygones and you're quite a catch."

"Am I really?" He watched her try to find a

way out of the situation and he had to clamp down to keep from grinning. "What makes me such a catch?"

"First off, you're a horrible person who likes to get a woman cornered and embarrass her." She had recovered. "On second thought, maybe you're a rotten catch."

"Try to remember that, please. Because if I was such a good catch…"

Now he'd gone too far, and the way she looked up at him, it made him want to kiss her again. And he really had to stop kissing Gracie Wilson. No matter how tempting that apple lip gloss she'd worn earlier or the sweet way she laughed.

He had too much going on in his life to be Gracie's rebound man. When he did decide to date, he wanted to know that he and the woman had a chance at forever. He had decided he was getting too old for random dating that went nowhere.

"I should go." He grabbed the box off the table.

"Patrick, I really do appreciate the help tonight."

"I was glad to do it. I'll see you at work tomorrow."

"Of course." She walked with him to the door. If she'd stayed in the doorway, it would have made things a lot easier for him. Instead she followed him out to the truck. He loaded the box of leftover supplies and turned to find her still next to him. The combination of moonlight, that apple lip gloss and the light scent of floral perfume could be a guy's undoing, even a guy who had perfectly decent intentions.

He opened his truck door. She took a step back.

"See you tomorrow." She smiled up at him as he got into his truck.

"You owe me lunch." He winked as he said it.

"I'll pick something up from The Everything."

"Perfect. Pizza?"

"Pizza."

He drove home lost in thought. The three blocks turned into two miles as he drove out of town, past the church that was now empty, then around by Bronson Park. He stopped at the remnants of the community garden. Coraline had told him the irrigation system seemed to have sprung a leak. He would have to get that fixed in the next few days. For now the water was turned off. The garden was in the last stages and they'd had plenty of rain.

Small-town life. He enjoyed it. Everyone

knew his name and his business. That was good and bad. But people cared.

He stopped his truck and leaned back to watch the full moon rise into the sky over a small town, fields of grain and corn, lonely houses stretching into the countryside.

His new world. The town he'd decided to risk everything for. There were things he was learning about himself in this town. But he still had a long way to go.

At lunch the next day, Gracie made her rounds. She stopped by the Fluff & Stuff pet store, browsing for more supplies for Rufus, who now lived at The Fixer-Upper with Patrick. She also bought the dog a great ball that could be filled with peanut butter. Chase Rollins was busy with a customer, so she waited until he was free to approach the counter.

The owner of the Fluff & Stuff smiled at her as she walked up with her arms full of goodies for the dog. She dumped it all and then stretched her arms to relieve the kinks.

"You know, I have baskets to put stuff in." Chase, the epitome of tall, dark and handsome, smiled his typical stiff smile. She liked him, even if he seemed a little tense at times. Maybe he really was in the witness-protection program and that was why he kept so detached. She liked the thought even if she knew how wrong it was.

"I didn't plan on getting this much," she explained, "but I kept seeing stuff Rufus would love."

"The stray?" He started ringing up her purchases.

"Yes. I think he likes Patrick. And Patrick seems to be okay with Rufus."

"Rufus, huh? Well, I'm glad he found a home." Chase told her the price and bagged the items. "I saw the truck dump him at the end of Main, on Granary. I tried to stop them but they took off. That poor dog stood there looking after them, probably wondering how the people who loved him so much could drive off and leave him on the side of the road."

"Do you wonder if they ever think about the dog, Chase? It kind of breaks my heart thinking about it. I'm glad he found his way to The Fixer-Upper."

"I don't think they do think about it, Gracie. But he ended up with a good home."

"Thanks." Gracie paid him and reached for the bag. "And the other reason I'm in here is to talk about the end-of-the-month block party. If you have a door prize, or door prizes, I'll put the list in the *Gazette*. And we'll also have a scavenger hunt for the grand prize, a carriage ride."

"I'd heard you'd arranged carriage rides."

"The money is going to the school." She glanced at her watch. She was running out of time. "We're promoting this to other communities. We're hoping to make it an annual event and include other towns. Each week we'll promote a different town and what they have to offer."

"What a great idea."

"I hope it works. We don't have as much to offer as a big city, but we're closer and buying local means supporting local schools and emergency services. And now, time for me to run. I still have to stop at a few of the other stores."

On her way down the block, she stopped by Allison True's bookstore but a sign on the door read Back in Fifteen Minutes. She hurried up the sidewalk to the Sweet Dreams Bakery. First she bought a fabulous cupcake and while she ate it she discussed the block party with store owner Melissa Sweeney.

"Oh, do you want to see a picture of the cake I'm making for Lily's wedding?" Melissa pulled out a book of photos.

"Of course."

Melissa gave her a cautious look. "Are you

sure it isn't too soon? I'm sorry, sometimes I don't think."

"No, really, it's okay. I want you to know my cake was beautiful. Not that I got to eat any of it. But I did hear that everyone loved it."

Melissa laughed a little and her cheeks turned pink. "It really was good. But promise me the next time you get married you'll put your foot down and get the cake you want."

"Vanilla with white icing. No strawberry jam, no almond extract."

"I'll remember that."

"I'm not planning on getting married anytime soon." Gracie glanced at the pictures of cakes and let herself dream just a little about a wedding that would be simple, with a groom who wouldn't break her heart. She swallowed, and when she looked up, Melissa was watching.

"Not all men break our hearts, Gracie."

"Who has a broken heart?" Gracie pointed to a beautiful cake with smooth, white icing and all the while wondered how Melissa had known what she'd been thinking. Was she that transparent? "That's my next cake."

"Perfect for you. And I'm saying you have a broken heart. But for whatever reason, you took the fall and let everyone label you the Runaway Bride. I'm not sure why you did that for him."

"Silly, I guess."

Melissa pointed to a three-tier cake. "This is Lily's cake."

"I love it." Gracie tossed her cupcake wrapper in the trash. "Oh, door prizes for the block party."

"I'm giving two. I'll give six cupcakes to each winner."

"Perfect."

"Oh, and the day of, I'm letting children decorate miniature cupcakes for free."

"I love that. Do I qualify as a child?"

"No, but I'll let you have one anyway."

"Thanks, Melissa. See you later." Gracie hurried out the door. Rather than head for the Cozy Cup Café, her next stop, she went down the street and around the corner to The Everything. The shop was just that, everything. The combination convenience store/gas station was a staple to Bygones. And the owners, Elwood and Velma Dill, were real characters. They ran the store wearing tie-dyed T-shirts. There were days both had their longish gray hair in ponytails.

Gracie hurried into the store, smiling at Velma, who was sitting behind the register reading a romance novel. She looked up, smiling a big smile. Gracie loved Elwood and Velma. They'd always been good to her.

As a young teen she used to walk down to The Everything from her dad's granary. She'd sit with Velma, who would tell her stories about all the places she and Elwood had traveled to and even lived. They had seen the world. They'd fed children in Africa and built homes in South America. And Velma had lost her mother at a young age.

Velma got the heartache, the constant empty space as milestones were achieved. Alone. Velma had been through some of those milestones with Gracie. Most people in town didn't know.

"Hey, sweetie, what has you rushing around town like a crazy person?" Velma put down her book and stood to lean over the counter.

"I'm making sure you're in on the block party."

Velma smiled at that. "Gracie, that's why I love you. Some people might forget us old folks with stores that have been here forever, but not you."

"The new stores are great, Velma, but you all have made a contribution to this town for years. You're loyal to the town, and the town is loyal to you."

"Well, of course we'll be involved in the block party. I think the Steins are going to keep their carriage here. They'll start out, go down Main Street, around the park and back here."

"Great. I'll make sure that's in the paper and on the map we're passing out."

Velma pulled a pack of chocolates off the rack. "These are for you. I know you love these."

Gracie blinked back tears and smiled at her friend. "Velma…"

They hadn't talked, not really, since the almost wedding. They had talked the week before. Gracie had gone to Velma with her fears, her concerns.

"Don't cry on me. You know I'll cry with you. Gracie, you did the right thing."

"I should have listened to you when we talked. I should have called the wedding off. I just didn't know how."

Velma patted her hand. "Don't beat yourself up. Someday you'll find the right man."

"I think I'll take a break from romance."

"That's not such a bad idea, either." Velma reached for one of the chocolates and popped it into her mouth. After a moment of thoughtful chewing, she smiled. "But I wouldn't write it off. The right man will make you forget all about Trent Morgan. The right man will help you trust."

"Thanks, Velma." Gracie finished the last

chocolate. "Oh, I have to get my pizza and head back to work."

"Speaking of…" Velma chuckled and walked off.

"Speaking of what?" Gracie called after her.

"You expect me to connect the dots for you." Velma boxed up the pizza and brought it back, sliding it onto the counter.

"Connect dots?" Gracie knew exactly what Velma meant but she wasn't going to bite.

"Ten dollars for the pizza, Gracie. And you know exactly what I meant."

Gracie knew, but she couldn't, wouldn't admit to the crush she had on her boss. It was too soon. She paid for the pizza and hurried from the store. What would Patrick think if he heard people talking about them?

She ran across the street and used the back door of The Fixer-Upper.

Patrick was in the stockroom going through one of the drawers full of nails. He turned as she walked in, smiling and then going back to his search.

"Looking for something?" She set the pizza on a worktable.

"I have an order for a couple of rocking chairs and I'm short on some parts."

"I thought we ordered those." She joined him, searching through drawers he hadn't searched.

"We did. They haven't shipped. There should be some here. Did you get everything done you needed to?"

"I think so. The block party is going to be a great success. And then in October we have the Fall Carnival."

"I think the more we do, the more we get people used to shopping locally, the better." He pulled out a couple of wood screws. "This is what I needed."

"Oh, good. Now you can eat lunch."

He glanced in the direction of the pizza. "Sounds good."

"Pepperoni and mushroom."

"My favorite." He slid the drawer back in. "Are you going to your church on Sunday? It's the Plainview Church, out past your dad's, right?"

"I think so. I don't want to abandon them now when so many people have left. I've only been going in town because the Morgans attend the Community Church." She didn't even like to think about what was happening, not just to her life, but to her town, her friends and now her church. "Our pastor thinks he might have to leave the area."

"That's rough."

"He's been with us for ten years."

"Maybe things will work out."

"We can only pray." The front door chimed to let them know they had a customer. Gracie pointed to the pizza. "I'll get that. You eat."

"What about your lunch?"

"I had a cupcake at the bakery and chocolates at The Everything. Other than a sugar rush, I'm good."

He laughed and she smiled back at him as she walked through the door and into the front of the store.

Allison True was standing in front of a display of shelves.

"Hi, Allison. How can I help you?" Gracie joined the woman who had grown up in Bygones but had left for several years. Now she owned the Happy Endings Bookstore.

Allison looked around the store. "I need some extra shelves for books. I'm on a limited budget, so I thought I could make some."

"We're going to do a workshop on bookcases. I have ready-to-assemble kits and then you stain or paint them the color you want. Do you want me to sign you up?"

"That would be great, Gracie." Allison looked around again. "You know, Helen over at the grocery store is really not behind the block party. I was over there a little while ago and she was complaining about the new shops."

"Oh, let her complain. She'll get over it when she sees that the new shops keep people in town and that will keep the grocery store going."

"I wish everyone could see it that way. I grew up in this town and I'm still getting it from a few people that I know."

"I'm sorry. I know it has to be tough. Especially if you came home thinking you'd get a nice, warm welcome from people you used to know." Gracie led Allison to the section of shelving and bookcases to show her the one they would be doing as a project. "They'll come around. It just takes time."

"It hasn't been easy, has it, Gracie? I mean, the situation with Trent, the wedding. Helen said that wedding was just another example of how this town has gotten carried away."

"I'm going to let Helen and everyone else in this town talk until they talk it out of their system. They really don't need explanations from me." She started to hum, an old habit for dealing with anger. She cleared her throat to cover up the sound.

Allison touched her arm. They'd never been particularly close, but things changed. Gracie thought that maybe they could be friends. She'd always liked Allison, but she'd left years ago. Even in school they'd been a grade apart and ran with a different crowd. But now, well, now was a different time. They were in different places.

"That's what they do, Gracie. They talk. But you're right, they'll get over it. Something else will happen. Maybe we'll have some good news or something else they can talk about. I need to get back to the store but if you need anything, I'm here. And sign me up for the workshop."

"I will, and thanks, Allison. Oh, and don't forget that Sam Franklin is going to be bringing the donation buckets for the Save Our Schools fund."

Allison nodded quickly and glanced toward the door. "I'll remember. But I'm not sure if I'll be in later today. I have some errands to run and no one to watch the store. If he comes by, can you get the bucket for me?"

"Sure. I'll bring it down to you in the morning. I'm sure he would deliver them earlier if he could, but he has to wait until school is out."

Sam Franklin had also grown up in Bygones and was now the school coach and father of twins. Gracie didn't know how he'd have enough time for fund-raising.

Allison had started to turn and walk away but

she faced Gracie again. "Coraline keeps telling me that the best relationships are built on a strong friendship. What do you think?"

"I think I'm definitely the wrong person to ask, but I can tell you that Trent never felt like a friend. I guess I didn't realize that until it was too late." Gracie smiled, letting Allison's unasked question go unanswered. Because to her it felt as if the whole world wanted to know if Patrick Fogerty was more than a friend and if he was the reason she hadn't gone through with her wedding to Trent.

If that was what people were thinking, then the best way to protect Patrick's reputation was to keep her distance and not give the good citizens of Bygones any reason to talk. And that was pretty hard to do, since he happened to be her boss.

Chapter Ten

Saturday after closing down shop for the day, Patrick headed for Mrs. Duncan's. He planned to start their project by power washing her siding even though they weren't schedule for major repairs or painting until Tuesday. A few people were going to join him to weed flower gardens and do some maintenance on the front porch where some boards were loose and a couple of posts were starting to rot.

He pulled up to the once-elegant Victorian and immediately spotted Gracie. She had a ladder up against the side of the house where English ivy was creeping into the siding. He'd brought weed killer, too. But the vines would have to come down before they could paint.

A couple of people from town were pulling weeds from the flower garden. Coraline Connolly stood nearby, supervising the project the way he'd learned only Coraline could. Around the corner came Mr. Randall.

Interesting. Some people in town blamed him for the current state of affairs in Bygones. Patrick liked the older gentleman, and like everyone else, he wondered what had pushed the owner of Randall Manufacturing to make choices that didn't make sense.

"Patrick." Whitney Leigh hurried across the lawn, a paintbrush in hand.

Behind her stood Josh Smith. Patrick needed to talk to him about those computer problems he was still having. For a guy with a coffee shop, he had a knack with technology.

"Whitney, are you ready to paint?" Patrick grinned past her at Josh, who was shaking his head.

"Of course I am. Your fellow city boy doesn't believe I can climb a ladder and paint at the same time. I told him it isn't as complicated as walking and chewing gum, and since he can do that, I can stand on a ladder and paint."

"I guess you probably can. I need to power wash the siding before we start painting, though. How are you at sanding?"

"I like sand." She smiled. "I especially like the sand on the Gulf Coast."

"I mean a sander on wood. The windows are

wood framed and the paint is peeling. We'll have to sand before we can paint."

"Oh."

She looked like a woman who had planned on a job that would be more fun than sanding. "Sorry."

"No, that's fine. I'll be back for painting and I'll sand today."

"Sounds great but again, I have to power wash first. What about the shed? You could start painting the trim on it. Since it's vinyl sided we won't paint the whole building."

"That's great." Whitney followed him back to his truck. He handed her a small ladder, a gallon of paint and a different brush.

"So, I just open it and go to work?" She looked at the can of paint as if it might jump up and grab her.

She wasn't a Gracie. But he liked her willingness to give this a shot.

Josh Smith stepped forward. "I'll help her out."

"Thanks."

He watched the two of them walk toward the shed and then pulled out the power washer and the new hose he'd brought, just in case Mrs. Duncan didn't have one. And he really doubted she did. As he hooked the washer up and then searched for an outlet to plug in the cord, Coraline Connolly joined him. Even working out here, she looked like a woman in charge. Her short hair, pantsuit and no-nonsense personality made her an authority figure no matter what she did.

"This is a great project, Patrick. You and Gracie are a good team."

He plugged in the washer and stood, turning to face a woman he'd come to respect in the few short months he'd lived in Bygones. He also knew what she was up to.

"Coraline, Gracie is just a friend." Why did he constantly have to defend their relationship?

She touched his arm with a well-manicured hand. "Oh, I know that. Of course I do. Stop listening to rumors—they'll drive you crazy. And make you defensive."

Heat crawled up his neck. "I know. I just hadn't planned on people linking the two of us."

"Of course they will. She works for you. You're a handsome single man and she is obviously still single."

Before he could respond, he heard Josh shout a warning. Patrick turned toward the shed just in time to see Whitney on the ladder reaching for the paint she'd set on top, above her head. It all happened in slow motion. Her reaching.

The paint toppling. He cringed as he watched Josh grab at the falling paint can with its aim on poor Whitney, his free hand shooting toward Whitney.

"Oh, that's bad." Coraline had covered her face with her hands but she peeked and then looked up at him. "Why did she have the paint on the top of the ladder?"

"That would be a good question but not one I'm going to ask." A dog ran through the yard, barking and joining the fray. "This could get insane."

Coraline started to say something but a scream erupted, stopping her. Gracie. Patrick turned in time to see the dog race under the ladder that Gracie was perched on. The ladder swayed. Gracie reached, trying to find something to hold herself steady. Her grasping hand found a vine but it snapped and she jumped to avoid falling with the ladder.

When Patrick reached her, she was flat out on the ground. The dog, a Labrador-looking thing, was licking her face.

"Gracie?" He knelt next to her, pushing the dog away. She opened her eyes and looked up at him.

"I think the ladder lost its footing."

"I think it did. Can you get up?"

"Of course. But I think I might need help. I landed on my foot and it's really throbbing." She smiled as she said it but a tear squeezed out and trickled down her cheek.

"Don't get up. Let me look."

"I need to sit up."

"Fine, sit up and let me look." He put his arm behind her shoulders and helped her to a sitting position.

"Patrick, I'm fine. I've been hurt worse."

"Okay, but I can still make sure you're okay."

"No, if you can help me to my truck, I'll just go home and put ice on it."

Coraline and several others had joined them. Coraline bent to look at the ankle Gracie wouldn't let him see. "Gracie, you're going to the clinic."

"I'm fine." Her face crumpled a little, because Coraline had spoken. He now saw that it took another hardheaded female to deal with the one in his employ.

"You're going to the clinic." Coraline stepped back. "Patrick, help her up and take her to get that ankle checked. The rest of us can finish the work here."

"You heard her." He reached for Gracie's hand but she didn't give it to him. Instead she managed to stand and then she hobbled away.

"You'll have to chase her down." Coraline walked next to him for a few feet. "She's used to taking care of herself. Her daddy loves her dearly but she's been the little mama at that house forever, and I think with all those rowdy boys, she got lost in the shuffle."

"I'll take care of her."

Coraline patted his arm. "I know you will."

He hurried after Gracie. She had stopped and was resting, leaning against a tree. He walked up behind her, placing a hand on her shoulder. She turned and half smiled but he could see the pain in her eyes.

"Allow me." He put an arm around her shoulder and scooped her into his arms, knowing she'd fight like a feral cat if he gave her a chance.

"Put me down." She wiggled to get free.

"Not on your life, Gracie Wilson. Coraline has given me my orders and I'm more afraid of her than I am of you. Besides, you don't weigh one hundred pounds soaking wet."

"You're not supposed to comment on a woman's weight."

"You'll survive." He grinned down at her and nearly tripped over a tree root. "Hold still or we'll both be in the E.R."

"I wasn't moving," she whispered, her lips quivering. No, she hadn't moved.

He held her tight in his arms and reached for the passenger door of his truck. If he kept his mind busy, he wouldn't kiss her. He wouldn't pull her close and hold her the way he wanted to hold her. Behind them were more than a half-dozen citizens of Bygones, all of them looking for something to talk about.

With that in mind, he settled Gracie in his truck, closed the door and walked around to the driver's side. When he got in, she was leaning back in the seat, her eyes closed. He reached for her hand, and her fingers closed around his.

"Don't tell my brothers."

"Okay." He started the truck and shifted into Reverse. "Why not?"

"Because they tend to take over. I really don't need them taking over."

"I won't call them. But you will have to let them know eventually."

She opened her eyes and smiled at him. A truck honked behind him and he slammed on the brakes, barely stopping in time to keep from getting hit by the truck passing on the road he was about to back onto.

"That was close." She laughed and her fingers remained on his. "I think I've really hurt myself this time."

"This time?"

"I guess I'm accident-prone, but I usually manage to escape injury."

"I'm glad you're telling me now. Maybe I should have put that question on the employment form?"

"Maybe you should have. But I'm usually very careful."

"Of course you are." He drove the few blocks to the clinic and parked.

Gracie reached for the door and he stopped her. "I'm coming around there to get you out. Stay where you are."

"Okay, fine. But I can take care of myself."

"I'm sure you can."

He reached for her door just as a truck pulled into the parking lot. A truck with at least two Wilson brothers inside. He opened the door and Gracie shook her head.

"Great, someone called them."

"They're your brothers and they were going to find out."

"Right, I know."

Before he could answer, the brothers bailed out of the truck they had parked just a few spaces away. They flashed him pretty serious looks and then zeroed in on Gracie.

"What happened?" The taller of the two shot

Patrick another look that pretty much put the blame on him.

"Jason, relax." Gracie smiled sweetly and Patrick guessed she'd had a lot of years dealing with the men of the Wilson family.

"Relax?" The other brother stepped forward. "We got a call from Sam Franklin telling us you fell off a ladder."

"Sam shouldn't have called, Caleb. I'm obviously fine. And I hope you didn't tell Dad."

"He knows but he's in Manhattan."

"Good." She reached for Patrick. "You can help me now."

"We're here. He can go."

Gracie pointed at her brother Jason. "I'm fine. You can go. I don't need the brothers Grimm here lurking and scaring everyone."

Jason laughed a little. "Brothers Grimm? Seriously?"

"Yes, because you're grim. And you look like a thundercloud. And sometimes you even scare me."

"Yeah, well, we're your family. We take care of each other."

"Right," she whispered with a soft edge to her tone that took Patrick and maybe her brothers by surprise.

Jason scratched his chin. "We do take care of you, Grace."

"I know you do." She slid down from the truck, landing on her right foot. "But now I'm taking care of myself. You guys go back to the granary and I'll let you know if I need anything."

Jason sighed and looked at Caleb, who shrugged. "Have you ever won an argument with her?"

"Nope." Jason moved back a step. "Patrick, she's all yours."

Patrick wanted to argue with what those words implied. Gracie wasn't his. She worked for him. She was a friend, one of the best he had in Bygones. But the brothers were walking away and he realized he might be taking the words a little too seriously.

"Let's get you inside." He scooped her up again and carried her into the clinic.

A little over an hour later, Gracie was sitting on the avocado-green sofa in her little house, her foot up on a pillow and Patrick Fogerty rummaging in her kitchen. She smiled as she closed her eyes and listened to him talk to himself about her kitchen and the lack of food.

"Do you eat anything other than chicken-noodle soup and peanut butter?"

"I do, sometimes."

"You do know how to cook, don't you?" He walked into the living room and sat down, making the armchair look ridiculously small.

Did she cook? She sighed and nodded. "Yes, I can cook. I choose not to. I've been cooking since I was…"

His sympathetic smiled melted her words and she shrugged.

"Since you were a kid."

"Ack, don't get that sad look in your eyes. Patrick, I'm a whole person. I'm not a child or someone who needs to be taken care of."

"Of course you aren't. You've been taking care of everyone else since you were a kid. So who took care of you?"

"Everyone did, of course. You saw my brothers."

"I saw that they're protective." He raised a hand. "I'm sorry, they're your brothers and I like them. I admit, though, I do feel a little threatened when they're around, but I like them."

She laughed at that. "Welcome to the club. Men that my brothers frighten."

"I'm not afraid of them. What happened to the other guys?"

"Most were too afraid to ask me out. Or to ask me out twice. What about you?"

"Am I brave enough to ask you out?" His eyes widened and she enjoyed the hint of red creeping under the five-o'clock shadow covering his cheeks.

"I just wondered. You didn't cower and run."

"I thought about it, but my legs were too weak from fear."

She laughed again, picturing Patrick with knees shaking in fear. It didn't match the man she knew. "No, sorry, I don't think you were afraid."

"No, I wasn't. But about cooking?"

"I don't plan on cooking real food for at least a month. I've cooked for my dad and brothers for more than a dozen years. For the next month I'm eating chicken soup and peanut-butter sandwiches."

He didn't respond, just sat there looking at her as if she might be the most pitiful thing he'd ever seen. And she definitely wasn't. She planned on enjoying soup and sandwiches.

A knock on the door kept her from telling him. "Come in."

The door opened. Coraline stepped in first and then Ann Mars. Patrick unfolded his tall frame and stood. She looked from him to her two friends.

"We came to check on you." Ann stepped forward, her gray hair in its typical knot wobbling to one side. She straightened the skirt of her floral dress. "How are you, honey?"

"I'm fine, Ann." Gracie pointed to her wrapped foot. "It's a bad sprain. A few days with my foot up and then I go back and they might put it in a brace or something."

"Land sakes." Ann took the seat Patrick had been sitting in. "Have you had dinner?"

"We were just discussing that."

"Were we really?" Coraline jumped into the conversation. "And what were we discussing?"

Gracie avoided looking at Patrick. "It seems I don't have food to cook. I thought I'd take a break from cooking."

Coraline sat at the end of the sofa, careful not to bump Gracie's foot. "Well, I don't blame you a bit. How about if Ann and I run over to The Everything and get the two of you something for dinner?"

Patrick coughed a little. "I should go."

Gracie gave him a look, hoping he wouldn't leave her to the two well-meaning ladies. He turned in time to see her look. She widened her eyes and he grinned.

"See you tomorrow, Gracie?" He headed for the door.

"Your paint. You left paint here." It was the only thing she could think of.

Both Ann and Coraline turned to look at her.

"Did I leave paint here?" Now he looked to be almost on the verge of laughing at her.

"I think you did." She ducked her head and looked his way again.

"I can get it tomorrow after church."

Coraline stood and motioned for Ann to join her. "We'll run to The Everything and get burgers. Patrick, you load up the paint, and if there's anything else Gracie needs, I bet you can help her out. We'll be back shortly."

And they were gone.

Gracie let out a deep breath. "You were going to ditch me."

"I thought you might prefer their company to mine."

"No, you thought it was funny to leave me to them. They would have been hovering, smothering me with attention…"

He sat down on the coffee table and she wondered if it could hold him.

"Don't look at the table like you think I'm going to make it collapse."

"It did creak."

"So did you when I said I was leaving. I'm not leaving, but you have to know that people are talking, saying you didn't go through with the wedding because there is something between us."

"I know." She closed her eyes. Her ankle throbbed, her back felt pretty bruised, and her heart was definitely shaken.

"Let me get you a glass of water and the pain meds."

She nodded but kept her eyes closed. She heard him stand, felt the brush of air as he moved away. But then he stopped and his hand touched her head, his fingers brushing her hair. She opened her eyes and he smiled.

"That felt good."

His fingers brushed through her hair again. She shivered at the touch, tender but something else, something she couldn't define. Her breath caught and she thought he might kiss her again. She'd thought a lot about his kiss, more than she should. When he walked away, she breathed a sigh of relief and disappointment.

"Will you sleep on the sofa tonight? I can bring you a blanket?" he called out from the kitchen.

"No, I'm good." She turned to watch him in the kitchen. His back was to her as he stood at the sink, washing the few dishes she hadn't done that morning. "Patrick, don't."

He looked over his shoulder but went back to the dishes. "Is there a reason you can't let me help you?"

"You've been stuck with me all day."

"That isn't a horrible thing, Gracie."

"It feels horrible. And I really don't want to put you in an awkward situation, having to defend yourself or our friendship."

He put a plate on the towel next to the sink and dried his hands before turning. Her heart froze and then hurried to catch up with its natural rhythm.

"Are you telling me to go?"

She nodded. "Yes. If you don't the whole town will have us paired up and married off."

"That would be bad." He gave her a long look as he crossed the room with a glass and her prescription. "You're right. I'll go."

"Thank you for today."

"You're welcome. And I'll stop by tomorrow to check on you."

"You don't have to."

"I want to, Gracie."

She nodded and he stepped close. When he leaned down she waited, but then he dropped a chaste kiss on her head and backed away.

"Good night, Gracie." He winked and headed for the door.

After he left she sank down into her pillow, pulling the afghan off the back of the couch to cover her face. What she felt for Patrick didn't make sense. Nothing really made sense. Her mind was saying to keep her distance; she'd just left a very complicated relationship.

Her heart was saying that Patrick Fogerty was someone too wonderful to miss out on.

Chapter Eleven

Patrick was heading out of church Sunday afternoon when Josh caught up with him. "Hey, how's Gracie?"

The two walked down the steps and headed for the parking lot. "I haven't talked to her today."

"Coraline said she has a bad sprain." Josh pulled car keys out of his pocket.

"Yes. I thought I'd…" Patrick stopped. He thought he'd not start rumors.

Josh waited but Patrick didn't want to fill in the blanks. He wasn't sure he had the right answer anyway.

"So how do you like life in Bygones?" Josh moved the conversation in a new direction. "Do you think you'll stay when your two years are up?"

"I can't imagine going back to the city. You?"

"I'm not sure I'm cut out for small-town life." Josh tossed his keys in the air, caught them and then glanced past Patrick. Patrick turned and watched as several local ladies headed for one car.

"A lot can change in two years." Patrick opened his truck door. "I'm going to head over to Mrs. Duncan's and see if I can get her house cleaned so we can start painting Tuesday. I feel bad for not getting more done yesterday."

"You had a good reason for leaving. Listen, I'm supposed to meet someone for lunch, but I'll join you over there in a bit. I'll bring my ladder. We'll keep Whitney Leigh away from the paint."

"I hope we can get through these projects without any more injuries or catastrophes."

"So do I." Josh glanced at his watch. "Okay, got to run. I'll see you over there in an hour."

Patrick ran by his place to change into work clothes and grab a sandwich and then he headed for Mrs. Duncan's. When he got there, he found a yard full of people, and the house had already been washed down. He got out of his truck and walked toward a few people having a picnic.

Standing shepherd over the group, as was his place, was Pastor Garman from the Community Church. He turned and waved, then brushed a hand over his nearly bald head. His smile was big and, as always, contagious.

Lily Farnsworth, owner of the Love in Bloom flower shop, was with the group and her fiancé, Tate Bronson. Patrick knew that time was precious to the couple, who would be getting married in less than three weeks. Their presence really struck him. The community was behind this project.

He kind of thought that this showed how much the town was starting to support the whole idea of reinventing Bygones. There had been times in the past few months when he had wondered, but seeing this group gathered together, it hit home that people were starting to see the vision for what they were doing.

They weren't trying to change the town. They were trying to preserve it for future generations.

He walked toward the group. Tate Bronson stood and held out a hand to Patrick. "Surprise."

Patrick took the offered hand. "A great surprise."

"We're talking about the block party and how to help Gracie, because it sounds like she won't be doing the running she's been doing."

"No, she won't. But I don't think this will slow her down or stop her from getting the event organized." He accepted a soda that Mrs. Garman handed him.

"Not at all." Pastor Garman jumped into the conversation. "If I know Gracie, this will make her all the more determined to prove she can be down but still get everything done."

"Which is why we all want to help her," Mrs. Garman added as she stood next to her husband.

Patrick nodded but the question rolling through his mind was, why did they all feel the need to tell *him?* And then he got it, because he wasn't always slow to get things. Gracie had tried to warn him that word was spreading fast, linking the two of them as a couple.

He should put a stop to it. But how would he look jumping into this crowd and telling them he wasn't dating Gracie Wilson? They were not, at all, a couple. He knew how it would sound. It would sound like a man putting up too much of a protest. Or a man who wasn't interested in a woman who appeared to be a favorite daughter of this small community. Either way, he would look bad.

"Where do we start?" Pastor Garman tossed a paper plate into the trash bag someone had opened.

"It looks like we're ready to start painting. I hadn't expected to get to it before Tuesday. But with all of this help, we'll get more than this house and the Parker house done by the end of the month." Patrick used that as a way out of a tricky conversation. He had Pastor Garman to thank.

The perfect plan fell apart because, within minutes of starting to paint, he had company. Gracie hobbled toward him, maneuvering crutches on the uneven lawn and looking less than happy with her situation.

"Gracie, you're supposed to be at home resting."

She glared at him. "I'm not really sure when you became my boss."

He cleared his throat and smiled. "I am your boss. And don't even think about sounding five and saying I'm not the boss of you."

She didn't look like someone who wanted to smile, but she did smile. "Well, you're not."

"No, I'm not." He looked past her, at the crowd of people, many of them working hard at pretending they weren't watching Patrick and Gracie. Several continued to rake leaves but cast an occasional glance his way. Another group stopped to talk.

"Worried about what they're saying?" Gracie smiled up at him. She took the brush from his hand, leaned on one crutch and started painting.

"Not at all." He turned his back to the crowd. "But I am worried that you're overdoing it."

She glanced his way and smiled. With even strokes she swiped paint down the length of the trim. Of course she did a good job—she was Gracie. He wondered if there was anything she couldn't do. He asked her and she laughed.

"I'm not much of a cook." She dipped the brush into paint again. "I mean, I can cook, but I don't enjoy it."

What did he say now? He watched her paint, a tiny woman with more determination that any ten women that he knew. He should make her go home, or at least sit down.

Instead he backed off and let her paint. He hadn't been friends with Gracie long, but he knew her well enough to guess she wouldn't want him to play big brother. He walked away, searching for another paintbrush. He found one and headed back to Gracie.

A truck pulled into the already crowded driveway. Gracie's dad got out of the truck and headed their way, a tight frown on his face. Next to him Gracie whispered, "Uh-oh."

"I just want it known that I am in no way responsible." Patrick kept painting but he smiled. Gracie laughed just a little.

"Gracie." Her dad's voice boomed. Patrick

had met Mr. Wilson a few times and knew him to be kind but gruff. He was a big man who seemed even bigger because of that loud voice.

"Dad." Gracie swiped more paint onto the trim.

"I went over to check on you but..."

"But I'm here painting."

Her dad cleared his throat and Patrick took the hint. "I'm going to go see if I can help with the plastic they're putting on the windows."

"Chicken," Gracie called out as he walked away.

Yes, he was a chicken. He didn't want to be the person responsible for taking care of Gracie. Not that Gracie wanted to be taken care of. He thought she could handle almost any situation, and she could definitely handle her dad.

He glanced back and he rethought that opinion of her. She looked small standing next to her dad. Bits and pieces of conversation floated his way. She appeared to be trying to convince her dad she was fine and she really could take care of herself.

Maybe he would find it easier to believe her if he hadn't been the one to find her the day of her wedding. The day she'd been sitting in the stockroom of his store, alone. Why hadn't she gone to someone, to a friend or a relative? Why had she gone to the store, by herself?

While he stood there trying to decide what to do next, Pastor Garman, tall, thin and always dressed for Sunday services, walked over to grab a drink out of a tub full of bottled water and cans of soda. He opened his bottle of water and reached for a couple of chocolate-chip cookies.

"Good crowd." Pastor Garman smiled at the people working, most of them members of his church. "Gracie is a tough young lady. I guess with all of those brothers she has to be."

"I suppose she does." Patrick let his gaze settle on the woman leaning on one crutch as she painted. Her dad had picked up the spare brush and was helping her. The two of them knew how to talk to each other.

He'd never had that with his own dad.

Pastor Garman had walked away, leaving him alone, watching Gracie. He realized what he'd been doing and reached for a couple of cookies, still distracted, still thinking about that moment when he'd found her sitting in back of The Fixer-Upper.

She'd been worried about how everything would affect her dad.

He headed across the lawn in the direction

of the father and daughter. Gracie glanced his way as her dad told her to go home and put her foot up. She shook her head and painted another section of window frame.

"Dad, I'm fine. I'm not moving. I'm not putting weight on it. I'll go home in an hour and put my foot up. Promise."

"Did you drive?" Mr. Wilson looked uncomfortable with the conversation. His neck turned a little red and he glanced across the yard as he spoke.

"I walked. Go home, Dad. You need a day off. Let the guys feed cattle tonight. Let Evan clean house. Take some time off and relax."

The older Wilson scratched his chin and smiled at his daughter. "You have to stop taking care of us. That means don't answer the call for help every time one of your brothers has a crisis."

"It's a hard habit to break."

"I know it is, honey, but we're good. We can clean. We can even cook when we have to. We have to break the habit of letting you do those things for us."

"I love you, Dad." She kissed her fingers and placed them on her dad's cheek. "I'll be fine."

"Okay, but don't overdo it."

He left. Patrick joined her at the window. "So, Gracie Wilson, who takes care of you?"

He wished he hadn't asked but the question slipped out and she looked at him with wide eyes.

"I take care of myself, Patrick."

He let it go. He had to. He still had enough sense left to know when to walk away.

"I'm going to check on the condition of the siding on the back of the house. I heard it's cracked."

"I'm not going anywhere."

"When you're ready to go home, let me know and I'll give you a ride."

She dipped the brush into the paint and shot him a look. "I guess you take care of me, Patrick."

He got the hint. "I'm going. But I mean it about the ride."

"I know. And I'll let you know when I'm ready to go."

He left, because it made good sense to walk away.

Gracie had hoped Patrick would forget he'd offered her a ride home. It would save them both a lot of trouble. He didn't forget. As everyone packed up to leave, he appeared at her side.

"Ready to go?"

She nodded and positioned the crutches under her arms again. She waved goodbye to a couple of people and walked with him to his truck.

"I really can walk."

In answer his dark brows lifted and he shook his head. He opened the truck door for her and waited until she had climbed inside. His hand was on her arm and she inhaled the clean scent of him mixed with outdoors.

As soon as she got home, she'd say her goodbyes and he would leave. Maybe she'd tell him he wasn't responsible for her. She didn't want that from him.

She didn't want him at her side because he felt as if she needed someone to take care of her. People did take care of her. Coraline and Ann had always looked out for her. Velma was a wonderful friend. She had her dad, even if he sometimes seemed uncomfortable or distracted.

Unfortunately she didn't make the clean break from Patrick. When they got to her place, he followed her up the sidewalk to her front door. She opened it and then turned to look up at him.

Her heart stumbled over the protests she'd been about to make. Instead her mouth went dry and she didn't know what to say.

"Gracie?"

The soft voice broke into the rush of emotions. She smiled at the man still standing on the stoop outside her house while she stood in the doorway with the screen door pushed open.

"I'm sorry. I was thinking."

"That you might need some help?"

"No, not really." She'd been thinking that he meant something to her, even if she wasn't quite ready to name what.

He filled up space in her heart in a way that took her by surprise. How could she let him in that way? She steadied her gaze on his face, wanting to believe that he would be the man who accepted her as she was.

But he wasn't asking to be that man.

"Let's go in. I'll get you an ice pack."

She moved and he stepped inside, motioning for her to sit down. She sank onto the old green sofa and sighed. While her eyes were closed, he moved around the room. A few minutes later, he lifted her foot and placed pillows under it. She opened her eyes and watched as he walked away.

When he came back, he had a bag of ice. He unwrapped her foot and placed the pack on her ankle. She cringed as the cold hit.

"Nice?" He grinned as he said it and she couldn't find a response. She could barely breathe. Her ankle hurt. Her heart ached. Breathing seemed overrated.

She nodded. He backed up, his hand slipping off her foot. He put distance between them, which seemed like a good idea to Gracie.

"Can I get you something to eat?"

Gracie grimaced at the offer. She moved her foot to a more comfortable position before answering, "I think you'll find that there isn't a lot to fix."

"I'll run down to The Everything. I can bring back a pizza."

"That would be a good rumor-starter."

"You know that we've already started rumors, right?"

Heat climbed into her cheeks and she nodded. "Yes, I know. It's your fault. You insisted on taking me to the clinic and then you brought me home this afternoon. People are going to draw conclusions. And worse."

"Worse?"

How did she tell him? Her heart hammered against her ribs.

"They think you're the reason I didn't go through with the wedding."

He sat down on the chair opposite her. "That's a new one."

"Still want to live in a small town?"

"Sometimes I wonder." He leaned forward. "I never thought that would be the rumor."

"No?"

She smiled as he thought about it. She enjoyed watching him think. She enjoyed the strength of his face and the way his dark eyes sometimes sought hers. There were times at work when something funny happened and he would turn to look at her with those eyes of his. It connected them.

Dangerous thoughts. She must be going through a time in her life when she felt a need to have someone, anyone, to lean on, to connect with. It wasn't about him or needing him.

Needing people hurt. She closed her eyes against a wave of emotion that was more than a decade old. Needing someone. She had needed her mom so much and so many times. She had needed her dad to see that she was hurting. Now, looking back, she realized he tried. He just hadn't been equipped to be a single dad with a houseful of boys and a lone daughter. He hadn't understood her emotions. Or her stubbornness that was so much like his own.

"You okay?" Patrick's voice was soft but husky. It skimmed across her, sending shivers up her arms.

"I'm good."

"Pizza?"

"Yes, pizza is good. But you don't have to."

"I know that." He pulled his phone out of his pocket and called The Everything to order pizza.

After the call, he stood and Gracie felt small and suddenly self-conscious. She looked up at him, watching as he pulled the afghan off the back of the chair he'd been sitting in. He settled it over her and she didn't know what to feel in that strange moment that could have been awkward but wasn't.

She reached for his hand and drew it to her cheek, holding it, strong and warm, against her skin. "Thank you."

He exhaled sharply. "Gracie."

Her name sounded drawn from deep down in his chest. He leaned down, the movement taking her by surprise. His hand slipped through her hair and he hovered then claimed her lips in a kiss that didn't surprise her. It tore loose the emotions she'd been holding so tight, so secret. It shredded her last defenses.

Somehow he was sitting next to her and she was leaning into the kiss as her arms went around his neck. Her hands settled in his soft, dark hair as he continued to hold her close, his lips firm and warm, his hands on her back strong.

Finally he pulled back but she didn't want

to lose the moment. Her hands remained on his shoulders and she rested her head against his chest. She heard the strong, steady beat of his heart.

"I should go." He moved a little and she released him.

"I know." Her voice shook and she didn't want to cry. She didn't want to need him this much. She didn't want him to know she needed him.

This wasn't the right time, not now when she was just getting her life back. She was just starting to find herself.

She didn't think it was the right time for him, either. She saw that in his eyes and in the way he drew back from her.

"I'm coming back." His hand held hers and he looked down at their intertwined fingers. She followed his gaze, wondering where his thoughts had gone and wishing she could ask.

"Patrick, I don't know what to do."

He stood, his fingers sliding loose from hers. "Me, neither."

"I don't want things to be awkward between us. I don't want to lose our friendship."

She wanted him to tell her they would always be friends and that he wouldn't leave, he wouldn't go back to Michigan. She didn't want to lose the person she drank coffee with in the mornings while they waited for customers or the man she discussed her crazy ideas with. She didn't want to lose the man who didn't laugh at the plans she made for the town, for his store.

She couldn't remember ever having someone in her life who listened to her the way he did. She couldn't imagine life in Bygones without him. Or her life without him.

The thought took her breath away.

"I'll be back in a few minutes." He walked out the door and left her alone to sift through the wild thoughts tumbling through her mind.

She whispered an okay as he left, but she didn't know if he heard. After he was gone, she cried. She didn't know why she cried. Maybe because of the pain. Or because Patrick's kiss had changed everything. She needed him in her life. With Patrick, for the first time in a long time, she didn't have to smile and pretend everything was okay.

Chapter Twelve

On Monday morning Gracie hobbled into the store, crutches gone. Patrick watched as she stored her purse in a cubby under a worktable and grabbed the green utility apron that hung on her tiny frame, well past her knees. He really needed to get one made that would fit her. He smiled and shook his head, knowing better than to say she should be at home.

"Good morning, Gracie." He finished attaching an armrest to the rocking chair he was working on.

"Patrick."

"You know you should be at home." He looked up only briefly. So much for not saying anything.

Should he bring up yesterday and the kiss that had left them eating dinner in silence when he returned?

"You know that I do what I want." She smiled

and leaned against the worktable. Her dark hair framed her elfin face, and her mouth turned up in that ever-present smile.

"Yes, I know you do what you want. Crutches for a week?"

"It's been almost a week."

"Half."

"Over a half." She stepped away from the worktable and finished wrapping the apron strings around her waist. He thought about his hands on her waist and kissing her.

Big mistake because he nearly hammered his thumb. It was time to put down the tools and get a cup of coffee.

"Want coffee?" he asked as he stepped toward the door.

"No, you go ahead. I'm going to clean up in here a little and then stock shelves."

"Gracie, you should really take it easy. At least for a few days."

"I'll keep that in mind."

He knew she wouldn't. As he started out the door, he glanced at the calendar and frowned. Great, he had a lunch date today. Just what he didn't need—another fix-up. Pastor Garman had arranged this one, with a nice young woman raised in church.

"What's wrong?" Gracie now stood next to him.

What did he say to her? So much for that less complicated, small-town life. So far he'd found nothing uncomplicated about living in Bygones. Well, maybe the lack of traffic. It was definitely easier to find a parking space. He didn't have to think long about where to eat lunch. He smiled at the run of thoughts.

"Nothing, just complications. Pastor Garman insisted I meet a nice young woman for lunch. We're meeting at Josh's for coffee and a sandwich."

"I thought I was the only one trying to find a woman for you."

"Obviously not." He pushed the door open. "I'm not sure how to convince you all that I recently turned thirty-five and I'm pretty capable of handling my own social life."

"I'm turning twenty-five at the end of the month and no one trusts me in that department."

He grinned and let the door close. "I can't imagine why."

"Funny." She brushed her hair back from her face. "But really, I think getting you married to a local girl is their way of keeping you here. If we can get all of the new shop owners married off…"

"Oh, so that's how it works?"

She nodded and her smile spread across her face. "That's how it works."

"I'm glad I know so I can avoid future attempts."

Her head cocked to the side and her eyes narrowed as she stared up at him. "Do you always avoid relationships, Mr. Fogerty?"

"Do you always play the part of the Runaway Bride of Bygones, Ms. Wilson?"

"Ouch." But she smiled and he knew that in the weeks since the failed wedding, she'd managed to get to the place where she could joke about the situation.

"I don't avoid relationships." He preferred to think of it as avoiding guilt because he'd never been able to put the time into relationships that they required.

Maybe it had been about finding a woman who made him want to put more time into a relationship.

She looked at the big clock on the wall. "Time to open. I have a workshop today."

"Oh, good, more single women."

They both laughed this time. He pushed the door open and she walked through, still limping, but obviously not listening to his advice or the doctor's.

"I'll turn the sign to Open," she offered.

"Thank you. And then you can sit behind the counter and look at sales for the month. I'd like to see if the discounts or your workshops are bringing in customers."

"You're taking it easy on me?" She unlocked the door and turned the sign. As she limped back to the counter, he saw a slight grimace that she quickly covered with a smile.

"Not at all. It's important to see what is working to bring in customers and what isn't. And I'd like to get prepared for the block party. I'm giving away a rocking chair. And by Saturday I'd like to have that website up and running so I can promote it to people who show up."

"Good idea." She took a seat on the stool behind the counter. "Where do I start?"

He reached next to her and pulled out the daily-sales logs. He placed it in front of her, leaning too close. His shoulder brushed hers and a faint tropical scent swirled up to greet him. He opened the book and pointed at the figures. Her dark hair fell forward in a softly scented curtain. She pushed it back with her hand.

"This is what I've been logging." He pointed to the different dates and the special events or promotions on that day. "I want to see if our sales figures are random or directly linked to any of the promotions we've tried. Advertising, special events, workshops, whatever."

"Gotcha. I'll go through and see what I can find. And really, I'm not going to sit here for the next week. I've got to talk to the different store owners about the block party. It's five days away."

"I know it's coming up. I've got to run out later. I'll go by and make sure the advertisement is going in the paper on Thursday. If you want, I can run errands and talk to the other shop owners. The ones I can't see in person, you can call."

She moved her finger across the ledger he'd been keeping sales totals written in. "Okay, that's good."

"That should keep you busy for a while. And when I go to lunch, I don't want you up trying to see how much you can get done while I'm gone."

She smiled at that. "I would never…"

"You would."

"I can't wait to hear how the date goes."

He ignored her teasing. "It isn't a date."

"Fine, it isn't a date." She hopped down from the stool and hobbled over to the coffeepot. She lifted it and he nodded. She poured two cups and handed him one.

"You never know, Patrick. The right woman is out there somewhere." She looked away, going back to the counter and the sales figures. But not before he saw a flash in her dark eyes. Why?

"Do you want to cancel your class for today?"

She glanced his way and shook her head. "No, I can teach it. Stop worrying about me."

Stop worrying. He agreed. She had been taking care of herself for a long time. Fortunately the customer that had come in was heading his way with a look on his face that said he needed assistance.

Patrick would gladly give the help needed if it got him out of the conversation that shouldn't have become so tense. But it had.

Gracie tried to pretend she didn't care when Patrick left for his lunch date. It shouldn't matter. He was her boss. He had a right to his privacy, and really, he didn't owe her any explanations. He told her he might not be back for a few hours. He had the list of people to talk to about the block party. All of the loose ends she'd planned to wrap up and hadn't been able to.

The Workshop for Women started two hours after he left. Gracie looked around the small group, smiling at the disappointed faces. Phyllis, present at the three previous workshops, appeared to be the most disappointed by his absence.

"I thought Patrick would be here. In case we have questions."

Allison True had shown up, hoping to put together bookcases for her store. She laughed at the question. "Why, Phyllis, do you doubt Gracie can answer your questions?"

"No, of course not. I mean, I know Gracie can handle anything."

Gracie cleared her throat. "Thank you for the vote of confidence."

Marilyn Parks leaned close. "Tell us the real reason you left Trent Morgan at the altar. Was it because of Patrick Fogerty?"

"Of course it wasn't."

Allison flipped brown hair over her shoulder and her blue eyes flashed as she focused on Marilyn. "That question was very unnecessary. Now, let's start thinking about these bookcases we're building. I don't have all day."

"Exactly, we're all busy and this is a lengthy project." Gracie grabbed the bookcase kit and sandpaper. "We'll start by sanding and then we can either stain or paint the wood, depending on what you want."

"When do we put the bookcase together?" Phyllis of the many questions asked. "And you have to admit your boss is cute."

"Yes, he is," Gracie answered offhandedly and kept working.

"So you are interested?" Marilyn asked.

"Seriously?" Allison sighed, a very long, drawn-out sigh. "Can't two people be friends without everyone going crazy in this town? Let's focus."

Focus. Gracie needed to focus. But her thoughts were traitorous and really did stray too often to her boss and to a kiss that had changed everything between them. Or at least it had for her. He didn't seem to be affected at all.

Maybe she should be thinking about Allison and what she'd just said, about two people being friends. Of course they could just be friends. She shot Allison a grateful smile and went on with the class. Each woman had questions about sanding and then about staining, the type of stain, the best type of paint. It didn't take long for the hour to pass once they really got started and focused on their project.

After everyone left and as she was cleaning up, she noticed that Allison had remained behind. "Hey, I didn't see you over there."

Allison stood next to the fall plants, staring at the window and at nothing really, it seemed. Gracie walked up behind her, placing a hand on

Allison's shoulder. She was taller than Gracie by quite a bit. She turned and smiled.

"Are you okay?"

Allison nodded. "It hasn't been easy coming home."

"No?"

Allison shook her head. "I've wanted to come home for years, but it never seemed like the right time. And now…" She shrugged. "I'm still not sure if I'm doing the right thing by being here."

"Is there anything I can do?"

Allison's gaze slid back to the window. Her blue eyes were shadowed and somber. "No, not really. Sometimes life is about accepting what happens, even if it hurts. Even if it doesn't make sense."

"True."

"I guess you know that better than anyone." Allison sighed. "I should go. I'm sorry for dumping this on you."

"You're talking to a friend, Allison. We all need people we can talk to."

"Yes, we do. I'm glad you're here, Gracie. I'm glad we're friends."

"And you'll remember that I'm here if you need to talk?"

Allison's smile returned. "It was just a moment and it's over now. But I know you're here."

Allison left and Gracie stood at the door watching her walk down the sidewalk. She wondered if someone had broken Allison's heart. Maybe it had happened recently, causing her to move home, to a safe place. Or maybe it had happened years ago, causing her to leave home. Gracie didn't know, and she wasn't going to go snooping into her friend's life. If Allison wanted her to know, she'd tell her.

Patrick came back thirty minutes later. As much as she wanted to know who he had met, she didn't ask. She didn't want to know if it had gone well and if he'd liked the latest blind date. Instead she took the cup of coffee and pastry he offered and she asked if he had talked to the police chief about the dunking tank they were going to have at the block party and again for the fall festival.

The school would also have several booths for the block party, including face painting. The school board had done some research on small private schools and how they raised funds for budget shortfalls, and some of the stay-at-home moms were going to sell different items through home parties, as well.

"What about the sales logs?" Patrick followed her back to the counter.

Gracie sat down and picked up the books she'd gone through earlier in the day.

"It seems to me that different sales and promotions bring in customers. But the women who attend the workshops also buy specific items, usually having to do with what they're making."

"Okay, that's good. What if we do a different sales promotion each week and advertise the workshops along with the promotion?"

"Good. I think that would work." She flipped through the pages again. "What if it doesn't?"

"I'm not sure. I don't have a business in Michigan to go home to. Maybe I could find a job somewhere managing a store."

"And leave?"

"It isn't my plan."

"I know it isn't."

The door chimed. Gracie glanced at her watch. She should have turned the sign to Closed. When she looked up, it was her dad. Her heart dropped as he walked up to the counter, looking unsure.

"Dad?"

"I thought maybe you'd have a few minutes to talk."

Gracie glanced at her watch and at Patrick, who nodded. "Sure, Dad, is everything okay?"

"Everything is fine. I just wanted to talk if we could."

"Patrick, I can close up."

Patrick looked at his watch. "I'll run upstairs and take our dog for a walk."

Their dog. She smiled at the joke. The stray had become the store dog, and lately, Patrick had decided Rufus could make his home in the loft apartment above the store. Patrick's apartment.

Patrick left and Gracie sat down, patting the stool next to hers for her dad. Her heart thumped hard as she waited, worrying about what he'd tell her. She'd had bad news before. Moments like this always sent her spiraling into the past when nine-year-old Gracie had sat in a doctor's office while the doctor explained to her parents that they couldn't help her mother. It was too late.

"Gracie, are you listening to me?"

She nodded and then she shook her head. "I'm sorry, I didn't listen. Daddy, are you okay?"

She shouldn't have moved out. She should have stayed home to take care of him, of her brothers. Her dad patted her leg and smiled.

"Gracie, calm down. I can hear your heart from here. I'm fine. Your brothers are fine."

"Okay, then what's wrong?"

"Can't a dad check on his daughter after she

moves out? You know we miss you. As a matter of fact, when this block party is over, I'd like for you to spend a Sunday with us. Maybe cook dinner?"

She smiled at that. "You wanted to talk so you could tell me you're starving without me at home?"

"No, that isn't why I came by." He let out a long sigh and his smile disappeared. She knew that now he'd tell her the bad news.

"Dad?"

"I wanted to tell you I'm going to sell some of our land. Maybe fifty acres. That affects you. It's yours, too."

"Dad, you do what you need to do to make things easier."

"Well, now, I know it will make things easier. But, Gracie, I've always thought we shouldn't rush into decisions like this. Sometimes God is getting ready to work and we rush in and solve the problem for Him."

"And make things worse?"

He smiled big and rubbed his chin. "And make them worse. I don't know what I'd do without you, Gracie."

"Well, you'd have a son-in-law right now."

"Not the right one."

"Oh, is there a right one?"

"For my girl? I'm not sure." He patted her arm. "You'll know him when you see him."

"I think I thought that once before and I was sadly mistaken."

"I think you wanted him to be the right one."

That didn't help her.

"Maybe so, Dad."

He stood and hugged her. "I'm going on back to the granary, but thanks, honey. I needed to talk this over with you. Your brothers listen but they'll do whatever I think is best."

"You've never let us down, Dad."

He kissed her cheek. "I try not to."

Her dad left. Gracie leaned her head on the countertop and sighed. If only everything could be so easy. A hand touched her back. She looked up, smiling at Patrick.

"I thought you left," she whispered, brushing the hair back from her face.

"I wanted to make sure you were okay."

"Oh." She was always okay. He should know that. Everyone knew that. "Of course I'm okay."

But his dark gaze remained on her face, studying her. He didn't think she was okay.

"I'm really okay," she repeated.

"Do you always say that?"

She smiled. "Yes."

Almost always. Usually she meant it. Today,

though, her heart felt bruised. If things had been different... She didn't want to go down that road, because things weren't different.

She also knew things would get better. As she walked out the back door of the store with her boss, she wondered how. Her dad was selling land that had been in her family for decades. The town she had grown up in was struggling to survive.

Her boss. She looked up at him as he opened her truck door. Somehow he had become the person she needed in her life. She hadn't expected that to happen.

She wouldn't make the same mistake twice, attaching herself to someone because she wanted it to be right. She had to stop thinking that sometimes, every now and then, he looked at her the way Tate Bronson looked at Lily, as if she meant everything to him.

This was the time in her life when she was finding out who she was and what she really wanted. Breathing the same air as Patrick Fogerty made that almost impossible, because he made her want to believe in the kind of love that took a person by surprise.

Chapter Thirteen

By Thursday Gracie's ankle felt as good as new. Almost. She walked around the outside of Miss Opal's house, wondering where they would start. For such a lovely lady, Miss Opal's house had gone downhill over the past while. Gracie knew that it had a lot to do with the death of her husband, Bobby.

Patrick walked up behind her. "This one might take time."

"I know." She looked the house over; from top to bottom it needed work. English ivy covered the siding, the flower gardens were overgrown and the front porch needed serious repairs. Fortunately the house had vinyl siding and didn't need to be painted.

"I'm going to order shingles for a few spots where it looks like her roof might leak." Patrick continued to look the house over. "How's the ankle?"

"Why, did you want me to get on another ladder?" She took the rake from his hand. "It's almost as good as new. I'll rake the weeds and leaves out of the flower beds."

"I'm going to get the ladder and start ripping those vines off the side of the house. Josh is going to cut the vines and spray the roots with weed killer."

A truck pulled into the drive. Gracie smiled when her brother Jason got out and walked her way. He surveyed the house and shook his head.

"Lost cause."

"Don't be so negative." She hugged him when he got to her and he lifted her off the ground a little. Jason always managed to be the brother who lifted her spirits. The two had stuck together over the years. But then Jason had moved to the old homestead, remodeling the two-bedroom home that had originally belonged to their great-grandparents.

"Hey, Patrick." Jason held out his hand to her boss. "Do you all need any help?"

"We can always use help. What's your pleasure? Pulling vines off the house, power washing, fixing that front porch? In a couple of weeks we'll patch up that roof."

"I'm a pretty good hand with porches." Jason lifted his tool belt, which showed he'd come prepared to work. "And Daniel should be here soon."

Daniel, closest to Gracie in age. She loved Daniel, but he spent more time studying and reading than had to be good for a person.

"That would be great. Your older brothers offered to help with the roofing project. They're both out of town, I think?"

"Yeah, they took some cattle up north. Someone said beef are bringing a little more in the Dakotas. I don't know if they could bring enough to cover the gas, but Caleb said if the buyers are going to give us rock bottom for cattle and sell them in the Dakotas for more, we'd just cut out the middleman."

"Makes sense if you can come out ahead on the deal." Patrick laughed. "Okay, I know nothing about cattle."

Jason pounded him on the back. "You'll learn. You can't live in Bygones and not learn a thing or two about farming. Or women."

"Women?" Patrick shook his head, clearly puzzled.

"I ran into The Everything for a burger and the ladies were discussing you."

"I think I should go." Gracie walked away,

because it suddenly hurt to hear that every single woman in town would like to date her boss.

The kiss. Her big mistake. Not her first or biggest. She tried to shake off what felt like a big dose of jealousy. She should know better. Patrick had made it pretty clear that he had no interest in settling down. She'd been the one trying to force his hand, to get him settled.

She put her jealousy to work raking leaves and dead weeds from an overgrown flower garden. Occasionally she had to yank vines from the mess of weeds. Someone walked up behind her as she yanked and pulled on a particularly difficult vine.

"That's a power cord." The man behind her finally spoke.

Gracie looked at the vine in her hand and cringed. "Oops."

She turned and smiled up at Police Chief Joe Sheridan. She shielded her face to block the sun and he moved to give her relief. It must be nice to be as tall as a mountain.

"Better?" he asked.

"Much, thank you." She leaned on the rake and lifted her foot to give her ankle a break. "How are you doing, Chief?"

"Good, Gracie. I thought I'd ask you the same. Seems you've had a run of bad luck lately. And last night someone decided to paint up the granary."

"They what?" She moved out of the house and suddenly her family didn't think she needed to know what was going on.

"Your dad didn't tell you?"

"No, he didn't."

Joe grinned, his face in shadows with the sun behind him. "Don't be too hard on him. I think his mind is a little preoccupied."

"Because he's dating. I think the empty nest, even if it isn't empty, is setting in and he realizes he has a lot of life to live." She could handle her dad dating. He probably should have dated sooner.

"I think so."

"But that isn't the reason we're talking."

Joe laughed a little. "Don't worry, nothing official. Your brother Evan hasn't pulled a caper in months. I wanted to make sure we've got our plan for Saturday's block party. I'm going to have the dunking tank set up over by the park. I think there will be booths on Main Street. The school and police department are both looking for every opportunity to raise money to keep us going. The fire department, too. They're volunteering to serve chili at the fire station Saturday evening."

"That sounds great, Joe."

"I hope this works, Gracie. I really don't want to cut the hours of any more of my guys. Or let anyone else go. What I really want is to bring back the guys who have left town and taken jobs elsewhere."

"I know. It hurts us all, doesn't it? They lose jobs, and then we deal with more crime, more vandalism. It's a shame we can't find someone to reopen Randall Manufacturing. A good business like that shouldn't just shut down."

Joe glanced around. "I know, Gracie. I guess we're all confused by that situation."

He stopped talking and glanced to his left. Gracie smiled as Josh Smith joined them. Joe was a great guy, but she sometimes thought he still had the idea that the new store owners were outsiders.

"Hey, Gracie, have you seen Patrick?"

Since when had she become Patrick Fogerty's keeper? she wanted to ask. But then she realized she worked for him, so people assumed she knew his whereabouts.

"Somewhere on a ladder pulling weeds off the house. Is there something I can do for you?"

"Do your many skills include wiring problems?" He smiled at the police chief. "Joe, I hope you know we're all behind the police force.

I really hope we bring in enough revenue to at least help the city a little."

"I know you do, Josh." Joe pushed his ball cap back. "It's a struggle right now. I know you come to the city council meetings, so you know the budget issues. They're talking about raising water bills, raising property taxes and even extending the city limits. Anything to bring in revenue. But the problem is, the people in town can't give any more."

"I know." Josh rubbed his cheek and sighed. "And we've got feelers out, looking for manufacturers needing a new location."

"I guess Mr. Randall is still considering selling the plant. Only time will tell." Joe shrugged. "I guess I should go. See you all Saturday, if not sooner. Gracie, good idea on this block party."

"Thanks, Joe." Gracie turned back to Josh. "And you're right, I'm definitely not an electrician. Patrick must be around the corner."

They walked together and found Patrick on the far side of the house pulling ivy out of the eaves. Gracie watched him, smiling as he worked. She admired him. He was good, kind and decent. That was all she felt, she told herself—admiration.

He was her boss. She couldn't fall in love, not now, not like this, with Patrick. A man who might or might not stay in Bygones. A man who was honest about not wanting a relationship. Her heart couldn't take any more. It had been trampled on by Trent. She'd trusted him and believed they would get married, have children and love each other forever.

Maybe her heart was the one who couldn't be trusted? It didn't seem to know right from wrong.

"There he is." She made the unnecessary comment and walked away, leaving Josh to talk to Patrick.

Leaving because she really had to get a grip and stop staring up at the man on the ladder with the perspiration-dampened shirt and dark hair glistening in the soft sunlight of early evening.

Patrick watched Gracie walk away and he wondered what had put that frown on her face. He hated the distance between them that had been growing for the past few days. It was his own doing. He'd kissed her. She was his employee. He felt the ladder shake and he looked down. Josh Smith's hand reached to steady it.

For a grown man, he sure knew how to walk into some messes. He had spent the better part of his life staying unattached and avoiding drama. He'd seen enough of it in his parents' marriage over the years. Constant turmoil had reigned in the Fogerty home during his growing-up years. He loved his folks but they hadn't known how to have a marriage.

"You coming down?" Josh called up to him.

"Yeah, sorry." He averted his gaze from the retreating back of Gracie Wilson. She didn't do drama. He knew that about her.

"What's up with Gracie?" Josh asked as Patrick landed on the ground next to him.

"I think there's a lot going on."

"Yeah, I guess there is. I saw the real-estate sign on a portion of her family land. That can't be easy." Josh walked with Patrick. "And the wedding thing. Do you think they'll eventually work it out?"

"I don't think so." He had wondered the same thing for a while, so he knew there had to be other people in town wondering if it had been a case of cold feet. He looked for Gracie as he and Josh walked. She'd moved to a new flower garden.

As he watched she pushed her hair back from her face and swiped her brow with the back of her gloved hand. She'd work all night if they let her. He smiled and looked away, only to find Josh watching him.

"She's lived a lot of life in twenty-five years," Josh offered.

"She's still young." Patrick had tried to avoid that thought, the age difference between them. He had tried to avoid a lot, actually. Like his overwhelming need to talk to her.

Josh laughed so loud several people turned to stare. Patrick shot him a look and walked away. Unfortunately, Josh followed.

"Patrick, seriously, man, you have to give up the island-unto-yourself routine."

"The what?" Patrick shook his head and picked up the sprayer of weed killer.

"You're an island. You came to this town thinking you'd start your little business and have a quiet little life in a small town. There's no such thing. Small towns are all community. And that equals people in your business."

"Great. That should have been on the information sheet when we signed up for this."

"Come on. You and I have talked. You know this is what you wanted. Maybe you'll get a piece of land and settle down here. You'll get married, have a couple of kids."

"Maybe so. And you're not going to stay?"

Josh shrugged off the question. "I don't know yet. Back to the problem at hand. I have some electrical problems in my back room."

"I thought we'd already solved that with the new lights."

"No, I think there's a bigger issue. I thought maybe you could give me a hand."

"I can. I'll trade you out. I'm trying to put together a website for my rocking chairs. I thought I'd add pages on the new businesses in town."

"I can help you with that. And more. If it's on the web, you want people to find it when they do searches."

"Yeah, I guess. That's where I'm lost."

"And I'm not."

"Why'd you come here, Josh?" Patrick had wondered more than a few times about his new friend who seemed to be stepping down a few notches to take up making coffee. "You could obviously work anywhere and not have to worry about creating a successful business."

"I needed a break from the rush of life. You know, I think we've both been there. You get busy and all of a sudden you realize your friends are married and settling down with families. You're still working fifteen hours a day with no social life."

"Yeah, I guess that's where I was."

"So, now we're here. Life is quiet. There's time for relationships and socializing."

"Yes, there is time."

Josh looked in the direction of Gracie Wilson. Patrick didn't look, not this time. She was young. She'd been in this town her entire life. She'd never traveled or seen much of the world.

Thanks to his mom, he'd been places and had experiences. She'd insisted. Thanks to those experiences, he knew where he wanted to be and what he wanted to do. Gracie Wilson seemed to still be searching for herself.

"I've got to run." Josh looked at his watch. "I've got an order coming in. The delivery truck broke down and he's running late."

"Do you need help?"

"No, I've got it. Hang in there, Patrick. I really feel like things will take off and these stores will survive."

"I hope they do." Because if his store didn't make it, he didn't know where he'd go or what he'd do. And it wasn't as if there were jobs in Bygones.

He waited until Josh left and he headed for Gracie, who was having a very long conversation with Opal Parker. The two were looking at a flower bed and Opal had knelt next to it, her hands motioning. Gracie joined the older lady, kneeling next to the jumble of weeds.

"Hi, ladies." He walked up behind them.

Gracie smiled up at him, her hand on the arm of the elderly Miss Opal.

"Patrick." Gracie moved weeds to show bulbs that were covered with a thin layer of dirt, leaving the tops exposed.

"I was just showing Gracie my lovely prayer garden. Each of these bulbs represents a prayer answered." She pointed to a climbing rosebush. "And my sweet husband planted that on our twenty-fifth anniversary."

"Those are wonderful memories, Miss Opal." Gracie leaned in close to the older woman. "I'll take special care to cover those bulbs."

"Thank you, dear. And I really appreciate all of you helping me this way."

"I'm glad we could help, Miss Opal." Patrick held out a hand to help the older woman to her feet.

She dusted her hands and hugged Gracie. "I'm going to go inside now. This air might not feel cool to you youngsters, but it chills me right to the bone. And Patrick Fogerty, you are a true gentleman."

"Thank you, Miss Opal." He offered her his arm and she took it and smiled back at Gracie.

After helping Miss Opal to her front door, Patrick found Gracie covering the prayer bulbs with straw that had been brought in for such projects. She tamped it down and straightened, placing her hands on the small of her back.

"She's quite a lady." He shoved his hands in his pockets to resist the temptation to put an arm around Gracie, who shivered a little as the breeze picked up. "And she's right about the cool air. I didn't notice it ten minutes ago."

"I'm ready for a cup of coffee and to call it a day." She looked west at the setting sun. "Not much more we can do now."

"I would invite myself over for a cup of coffee, but I think we're avoiding giving the impression that people have something to talk about."

Gracie shrugged it off. "I'm kind of beyond caring what people say. Once you've been the Bygones Runaway Bride, what more is there to talk about?"

"I think you might have a point."

"I have lunch meat that isn't sour and bread that isn't green," she offered, and they both laughed at the memory of his not-so-long-ago offer.

"Sounds…appetizing?"

"You can put chips on your sandwich. That makes everything better."

Thirty minutes later, he agreed. He'd never had chips on a bologna sandwich, but it did make it better. From across the table, Gracie pushed the bag of chips his way.

"More?" she offered.

He shook his head. "I think I'm good."

Relaxed. He sat back in the chair that hadn't been made for a man his size. It was a miniature designed for a small dining room. He felt like a giant in this tiny house, sitting across from five-foot-tall Gracie.

He'd been a man of faith since his early teen years, but here in Bygones he was learning more about himself and his faith. He was learning that sometimes a person had to relax and trust that the God who created the world could handle everyday problems. He'd learned that sometimes a person had to make a tough choice and pray for the best.

Sitting across from Gracie, he learned that it was good to take time to enjoy the simple things in life. *Simple* meaning bologna sandwiches and chips. *Simple* meaning a quiet evening sitting with a woman who loved life.

"What was it like growing up in Michigan?" She wiped her hands on a napkin and tossed it, with her paper plate, into the trash.

"Busy." He knew she wanted more than that. "I grew up in an affluent neighborhood. My family business had prospered for years and my parents enjoyed that prosperity. My mother enjoyed it more than my father. He worked long hours and we went on vacations without him."

His father had cheated on Patrick's mother. For years. He didn't want to think about that part of his life, his story. He had loved his dad and he'd respected him. It had hurt to find out about the woman he'd had a relationship with. It had hurt because she attended his father's funeral, robbing Patrick's mother of her time to grieve and instead turning grief into anger and bitterness.

"Patrick?" Gracie reached across the table, resting her hand on his. "I'm sorry, I shouldn't have asked."

He shook his head to clear his thoughts and somehow found himself brushing his thumb across her fingers, studying the pale pink of her nail polish and the soft silkiness of her skin. This was how a man fell.

But what did he do once he fell? He didn't want to be the next man to break Gracie Wilson's heart.

"I should go."

"Should you?" Her eyes narrowed. She pulled her hand back from his. "Maybe you should."

They stood at the same time, the action putting them front and center into each other's space. Patrick touched Gracie's face, running his fingers down her cheek. Her breathing stilled.

Yes, he should go. "I'll see you tomorrow."

She nodded, and as he walked to the door, she remained in the spot he'd left her. He couldn't remember any other moment in his life that made him want to stay with a woman more than that one.

And that woman, just weeks ago, had planned on marrying another man. Life didn't move that fast, did it?

Chapter Fourteen

Friday, the day before the block party, Gracie was still trying to make sure all of the loose ends were tied up. This had to work. For the sake of the business owners and her town, this block party needed to bring in new customers, the people who generally drove to larger towns and bypassed their own small town.

"Stop worrying." Coraline had been looking at stencils for a room she was painting. "My goodness, Gracie, you'd think someone was about to give birth."

Gracie smiled at that. "It feels a little like birth. This event is important to the stores."

"I know it is, but you have to trust God in this. It's going to be what it's going to be and there's no changing that."

"You're right. I know you're right." Gracie

saw a flash of dark blue and looked out the window. "What's he doing in town?"

Coraline turned to look out the window. "Land sakes, that man is like a bad penny."

"I think I'm going to turn the sign to Closed and head home." She looked at the clock above the counter. "It's time and I'm not going to stick around to see if he's coming in the store."

"Where's Patrick?" Coraline asked as she headed for the front door. "I'll get these stencils tomorrow. Put them on the counter with my name on them."

"I will. And Patrick took Rufus to the vet for shots."

"He was here when the workshop started, wasn't he?"

"Yes." Gracie had to wonder where the conversation was going but she didn't want to ask.

"The women do love that man. I think because he fits that 'tall, dark and handsome' thing to a T. And my goodness, the look in your eyes when they flirt."

"Miss Coraline!" Gracie gasped and then put palms to her heated cheeks.

"Oh, Gracie, you look pretty when you blush." Miss Coraline leaned in and kissed her cheek. "Do not let Trent bother you. He was a picture of perfect righteous indignation standing in the front of the church waiting for you. He simply couldn't believe you'd leave him at the altar. He thought he was too good for you, Gracie, and that you should adore him for marrying you. He isn't nearly good enough for you."

"Thank you." Gracie felt the heat climb into her cheeks again.

"See you tomorrow, honey."

Gracie locked the door after Coraline left and she hurried back to close out and lock up the register. She saw Trent drive past again. Maybe he would leave town before she went out to get into her truck.

Her plan to escape unraveled. She cranked and cranked but her old truck wouldn't start. She sat for a minute, giving it time to rest. It still wouldn't start. Her only option was to walk home. Instead she hurried back into the store.

She was sitting in the store room when the back door opened. She looked up, smiling, expecting Patrick. Trent walked in, looking smug and not as handsome as she'd once thought.

"What are you doing in here?" She reached into her purse for her phone.

"I wanted to thank you for ruining my life."

"I ruined your life? How is that, Trent?"

"Because my parents know why you didn't go through with the wedding and they blame me."

"Oh, and you were blameless? Trent, I have let everyone in this town talk about me. The stories range from my having an affair with Patrick Fogerty to my being fickle and not knowing what I want. Some people think I have cold feet and we'll get back together. You are the victim in all of the stories. So how has this ruined your life?"

"Because you made me look like a fool."

"You're the one who cheated on me. I kept it to myself, thinking I could get past it and that I'd trust you again. But then she texted you and I knew that marriage to you would be a mistake."

"We could have worked it out."

"If I loved you, really loved you, maybe I would want to work it out. Maybe I did love you in the beginning, but love isn't something you abuse, Trent. It isn't something you take advantage of. I hadn't realized it until recently, but I fell out of love with you a long time ago."

The back door creaked open. Gracie's heart raced and she froze. Patrick walked through the door. He looked at her, a long look that she didn't want to interpret because it might hurt. He turned his attention to Trent Morgan.

"You can leave my store." Patrick stood a good six inches taller than Trent. Gracie watched as her ex-fiancé exited the building and then she slumped in the chair.

When she looked up, Patrick was leaning against the worktable watching her. She saw what she hadn't wanted to see in his eyes, sympathy.

"I should go home."

"He cheated on you, and you let people think that you had cold feet? Why would you do that?"

She shrugged it off. "I really don't know. And what's more embarrassing—cold feet or the fact that he didn't even wait until we were married to cheat?"

"You deserve better." Patrick handed her the purse she'd left on the worktable.

"Thank you. I like to think I do. But so far..."

"So far?" He opened the door for her.

"So far I've got a horrible record in the romance department. And really, this isn't a conversation I want to have with you."

"I see. But you should know that I understand. I think the last woman I dated thought I was having an affair, but the only one I saw more than her was the store I was trying to save."

"We do what we have to do, Patrick." She looked away for a brief moment. "My truck won't start."

"Let me give you a ride."

"I don't mind walking."

He opened his truck door and motioned her in.

"Let me give you a ride."

She nodded and climbed in ahead of him, scooting to the passenger side and buckling her seat belt.

"Thank you for coming to my rescue, again. It's becoming a habit."

"I don't mind." He started the truck and pulled onto the road. "So, you're not going to work things out with Trent?"

The question came from nowhere. She laughed and it felt good to laugh. "No, I think it is safe to say we won't be working things out."

"I'm sorry."

She wasn't.

When they got to her house, he walked her up the sidewalk. She turned the key in the lock and pushed the front door open.

"Do you want a cup of coffee or glass of tea?" She stepped inside. He didn't follow her.

"No, I think I shouldn't come in tonight." He rested a hand on the door frame and leaned in, dropping an easy kiss on her lips.

A few minutes later, she watched as he drove down the road, and she didn't know what to think about the easy goodbye that made them seem like friends.

Patrick parked in his space behind the row of buildings on Main Street. As he got out, another truck pulled up behind his. He waved to the man getting out. He couldn't tell Gracie's twin brothers apart, although she assured him the two men weren't identical. So this was either Caleb or Max Wilson.

"Caleb." The young man smiled big. "I could see that look in your eyes, the one that said you were going to have to say something and you had no clue what to say or who you were talking to. We're used to it, even though we don't see how people could be confused. I'm obviously taller and better-looking than my brother."

"Caleb." Patrick held his hand out. Caleb grabbed his hand in an equally firm handshake. "How can I help you?"

"I was looking for Gracie."

"She's at home."

"Oh, I saw that her truck is still here."

Patrick glanced at the truck parked in front of his and he groaned. "If you saw it, then how many other people have seen it and wonder if she's here?"

"She's really not here?" Caleb grinned and leaned an elbow against the back of his truck.

"Her truck wouldn't start."

"Then I'm going to make a suggestion that we get it started and take it to her place. If we don't, by morning the rumors are going to be a lot worse than they already are."

"I've been trying to keep my distance so people know that we have nothing more than a working relationship." He reached into the back of his truck for a toolbox.

"Right, of course." Caleb didn't seem to be buying it any more than Patrick was. He followed Patrick to Gracie's truck and reached under the front bumper to pull out a hidden key. "I don't know why she bothers pretending this is hidden."

Patrick shook his head and motioned for her brother to try starting the truck. Caleb got behind the wheel and gave it a shot. The engine cranked but didn't turn over. He looked the battery over, wiggled the cables to make sure they had a good connection and told Caleb to give it another try.

Nothing. He walked around to the cab and leaned in to look at the gauges. "Caleb, do you think she might have let this thing run out of gas?"

Caleb laughed and shook his head. "Yep. It wouldn't be the first time."

"I've got a five-gallon can of gas. Let's give that a shot."

He got the gas can out of the back of his truck

and poured it into the tank. The next time Caleb tried the engine, it sputtered to life. Patrick closed the door.

"Drive it home. I'll follow and give you a ride back."

Crisis averted.

"I can walk back from her place," Caleb offered.

"I don't mind giving you a lift. I wanted to." He had to admit it. "I thought I might check on her. Trent came by earlier."

"You know she doesn't like people getting in her business."

"Yeah, I kind of guessed that."

Caleb shifted into Drive. "Suit yourself. I'll meet you over there."

A few minutes later they were parking in front of the little house that Gracie had turned into her own in just the past couple of weeks. Even the outside had her personal touches. There were bird feeders, mums and a clothesline.

Gracie walked out as they were getting out of their trucks. Caleb walked up and handed her the extra set of keys. Patrick followed.

"You got it started." She smiled at her brother. When she looked at Patrick, the smile faded. "Thank you."

Caleb, a good foot taller than his sister, leaned down and picked her up. "It was out of gas."

"Put me down. This was fun when I was sixteen. Now it's just humiliating."

"Sorry." Caleb put her back on her feet. "I forget sometimes that you're not my little sister anymore."

"I'm still your little sister. I just don't like to be picked up."

"Gotcha, sis. Keep an eye on the gas gauge. You won't always have two handsome guys to rescue you."

"I'm pretty good at taking care of myself."

"I know you are." His tone changed. "But did you think how it would look to have your truck parked at Patrick's all night?"

She turned pink. "Great, that's not the fuel I wanted to add to the fire."

"No, it isn't." Caleb wrapped a protective arm around her shoulders. "Not that I would let anyone talk about my little sister."

"Do not lift me up again."

"I wouldn't dream of it. We're going to head back to The Fixer-Upper so I can get my truck. I have a date tonight."

"You?" She grimaced. "Poor girl."

"Lucky girl—we're going to a nice restaurant in Manhattan. Hey, if you see Dad, see if you can talk some sense into him. He doesn't have to put that land up for sale. I've got a savings account and I told him it's enough to get us through until things get better."

"You know he isn't taking your money."

"Yeah, I know." He glanced at his watch. "Okay, I'm running late. Later, sis."

"Later. And, Patrick, thank you." She smiled at him this time. He'd never known that a smile could make all the difference. In this case, it did.

Chapter Fifteen

Gracie walked down the crowded sidewalk from the Cozy Cup Café across Bronson Avenue and then the short distance to The Fixer-Upper. On her way she peeked into the other stores. Sweet Dreams Bakery had a long line, nearly to the door. The Love in Bloom flower shop had a small group looking at flower arrangements. The Happy Endings Bookstore had several customers browsing the new selection of books.

A carriage pulled by a big chestnut, its coat deep red in the midmorning sunshine, rolled down Main Street. The horse's hooves clip-clopped on the paved street.

She stopped to watch, taking a sip of coffee as people walked past her. Across the street, Ann Mars stepped out of This 'N' That and waved big. She'd had customers in and out of her store since she opened two hours earlier.

Gracie felt more hopeful than she had in months. She turned and bumped into Whitney Leigh. "Gracie, got a minute to grab a pastry from the bakery?"

"I think I might. Patrick brought in extra help for the day, one of the teenagers from church."

"That's good. I hope he needs the extra help."

"Me, too. I hope all the stores find that they could have used extra help."

Gracie followed Whitney into the bakery and she knew this wasn't a social visit. Whitney seemed to be reporter Whitney today. Hair pulled back and phone in hand, she looked like someone with questions.

"So, what do you really want, Whitney? I know the pastries at Sweet Dreams are wonderful, but you have your notebook."

Whitney smiled as she walked up to the counter and ordered two wonderful-looking cinnamon rolls. She turned and handed one to Gracie.

"I thought we'd talk about the block party and your role in putting it together. It's obviously a success. I've talked to people who drove up to thirty miles to get here."

"That's wonderful." Gracie couldn't have meant it more. She had been praying that this block party would be a success. Others were praying, too. "Too bad we can't convince Mr. Randall to open back up."

"That would definitely be an answer to prayer. Even if the plant could be sold to a company that would put people back to work, it would do a lot to help Bygones."

Gracie chewed a bite of the cinnamon roll before answering, "I know Mr. Randall's hurting, and I know the economy had hurt business. It's just hard to understand why he decided to just give up. It makes me wonder if the divorce is the reason."

"It makes me wonder if he's the man behind the revitalization of Main Street." Whitney's eyes narrowed. "And as much as I want to continue this conversation, there's Mr. Randall now."

"Don't be too hard on him, Whitney."

Gracie got a finger wave from the other woman as she rushed outside to catch the owner of the closed Randall Manufacturing. Gracie doubted Robert Randall would be getting any breaks today.

Gracie finished off her cinnamon roll, keeping track of the time she'd been gone. She was sipping coffee when Whitney returned, smiling as she led Robert Randall to a corner table, just behind Gracie.

"Mr. Randall, I really just want to ask you a few questions that everyone in town is needing answers to." Whitney was in full reporter mode.

Gracie felt a huge dose of sympathy for him, and probably the same curiosity everyone in town felt. Of course Randall Manufacturing had struggled, but did the plant really have to close down? Could time have changed anything? She sometimes wondered if he had put the money into the Main Street renovation just to ease the guilt he felt.

She also wondered why Coraline Connolly had paced by the window several times since he had walked into the bakery.

"Whitney, I really don't want to answer questions. Look at what this town is accomplishing, what the people are doing out there." Robert Randall sounded tired to Gracie.

Gracie wondered if he might have been suffering.

"Would you consider reopening, Mr. Randall?" Whitney asked. "To save the school and other public services?"

Robert Randall gave a long, drawn-out sigh. "I might consider moving far, far away so that these questions will stop. And that's saying something, Whitney Leigh. I don't want to leave my hometown. My answer is the same as ever—the economic downturn hurt us all."

The door opened. Coraline Connolly stepped in, her short gray hair styled to perfection, her pantsuit immaculate. "Whitney Leigh, there you are. I've been looking for you. I wanted you to write up a short story about the school fund-raisers through private companies and local representatives. We have home decor, candles, jewelry and even kitchenware."

"I'll be right there, Miss Connolly." Whitney's chair scraped back and Gracie knew that the interview would end now. It took a strong person to refuse Coraline Connolly.

Gracie turned in her seat to watch the two women walk away. She made eye contact with Robert Randall and he smiled but looked more than a little sad.

"It'll all work out, Mr. Randall."

He smiled a little. "I hope so, Gracie. I really do hope that things work out. I heard today that they're letting two more teachers go, and they still don't believe that will save the school."

Gracie's heart ached at the news. If the school closed, half the people in town would move and then the stores would have to close. And then what?

The plant was sitting idle. The machinery was

still in place. It would mean so much to everyone to have it reopen. But the way he looked at her, it was as if he were pleading with her not to say it. Of course she wouldn't.

"Winter's coming. I think if I was to travel, I'd go somewhere warm. To the beach. I've never been, you know." She smiled at the older gentleman.

"I'm afraid if I got to the beach, Gracie, I wouldn't come back. And maybe that's the way it should be."

"We would all miss you." She stood because she really had to get back to work.

"You should go to the beach, Gracie." He stood when she stood, a dapper man in a nicely cut suit. "And don't let people hurt you with their words. You hold on to the faith that has always held you up."

She hugged him. "Thank you, Mr. Randall."

She hurried away, not wanting to cry in front of him. As she walked toward The Fixer-Upper, she swiped at the tears that threatened to fall and pasted on a smile. There were customers out front. A few men sat in rocking chairs. Women looked at the bird feeders. Another horse-drawn carriage went down Main Street. A couple sat close while the driver talked, glancing back from time to time.

Patrick walked out the door, smiling at her as she walked up to a customer who seemed to be interested in a rocking chair. The man turned the chair, admiring the craftsmanship.

"Can I help you?" She stepped close to the customer. He looked up and then went back to studying the rockers on the chair.

"I'm impressed. Good craftsmanship. Does he ship?"

"Yes, sir, he does."

Patrick walked back inside, leaving her to take care of the customer. She could see that inside the store had plenty of patrons to keep Patrick and their young helper, Jeff, busy. The boy was in high school and knew enough about home repair to be a pretty good hand.

"I'd like to go find my wife and have her look at these chairs." The customer straightened and was looking down the street, probably for his missing wife. "I think we'll probably take two of them."

"We'll be here until five-thirty."

"Hi, Gracie, do you have your names for the first drawing?" Coraline Connolly walked up behind her. "We'll announce names of each drawing from the PA system. Josh got the speakers all hooked up last night."

"Yes, let's go inside. I'm sure we have names. How is everyone else doing?"

Coraline smiled big. "Oh, honey, this is going so well. I know one event won't save our town, but we're building something good here."

"Coraline, did you...?"

Gracie had told herself she wouldn't ask Coraline if she was the mystery benefactor responsible for the revitalized downtown of Bygones and the new stores. Coraline smiled at her.

"Now, Gracie, you know better."

"I know that you're a terrific lady who loves this town."

"Yes, I do love Bygones. So many of us do." Coraline patted her arm. "I'm going to get those names from Patrick. And it looks as if you have another customer."

She watched Coraline walk through the door and she turned to help the customer. She smiled at the man and his wife. He had come back for his rocking chairs. A commotion down the sidewalk drew her attention.

"Uh-oh." She jumped back

The customers moved out of the way. Sam Franklin, high-school basketball coach and math teacher, was chasing his twins, who were racing on what appeared to be stick ponies. Sam looked exhausted. But three-year-old twins of a boy-and-girl variety could do that to a man, or a woman, Gracie thought.

The three of them, and the two stick horses, ended their journey down the sidewalk at Sweet Dreams Bakery.

Gracie turned her attention back to the customers. Jake and Martha lived twenty miles away. They were having a wonderful time in Bygones and promised the next time they needed supplies, a book or even something for their animals, they would come to Bygones.

Gracie wrote up the order for two chairs and put a sold sign on the naturally stained rockers the couple had picked. She sent them inside to pay Patrick for their purchase and arrange pickup early the following week.

The block party had the makings of a great success.

Finally there was a lull in customers. Patrick walked outside. Gracie was rearranging the bird feeders and rocking chairs that hadn't been sold.

"This has been a good day." He watched as customers still went in and out of stores, drawn by great prices and the promise of door prizes.

"It has." Gracie sat down on one of the rocking chairs.

"Are you okay?"

She looked up, brushing wind-whipped hair from her face. "Of course I am."

"Your ankle?" He sat down next to her. It felt odd, the two of them in rocking chairs side by side. It also felt strangely right.

"It's a little sore," she finally admitted. "I haven't really paid attention until now."

"You need to take a break now that the rush is over."

"I don't think it's completely over. We still have two hours." She glanced at her watch and then at him. "Did you eat lunch?"

"No. I'm going to run down to the Cozy Cup and grab coffee. Maybe I'll stop by the bakery."

They rocked a few more minutes. "Patrick, I'm fixing dinner tomorrow. For my dad and brothers. Would you like to join us at the farm after church?"

The invitation took him by surprise. It made him think about what he was doing here and what she was doing. He couldn't think of another woman who had ever made him think about life as a couple. But he couldn't say that to her, not yet. Not weeks after she ended an engagement. How did he say that when she'd had a seriously failed relationship with a man who hadn't been what she needed?

How did he caution her to slow down, because he might not be what she needed?

"So?" She continued to rock, looking his way only briefly. "I'm starting to get nervous. Don't leave me hanging. I know I'm not the best cook, but I promise it won't kill you."

He smiled at that. "Maybe I should bring the bologna and a bag of chips?"

"Is that a yes?"

"That's a yes." He pushed himself up from the rocking chair. "I'm going to take a walk around the block and see how the other stores have done."

"I'll hold down the fort here."

He smiled back at her as he walked away. "Thanks."

He headed for the Cozy Cup Café and the coffee he'd been thinking about for the past few hours, since he'd emptied the pot of pretty bad coffee he'd made earlier in the day.

As he passed the Fluff & Stuff pet store, Chase Rollins stepped out. The guy was nearly as tall as Patrick.

"Patrick, has it been a good day for you?"

"Really good, Chase. People didn't realize what we had here in town. I think it's a great way to show them."

Chase nodded and looked down the street. "I

heard some of the locals talking when I ran over to The Everything to grab lunch. Velma settled things, told them the new stores are good for the community, but some of them think the town doesn't need coffee shops and pet stores."

Patrick had heard the same grumblings from time to time. "I guess there are going to be those people, Chase. But in time I think they'll start to accept us as part of the community. When they see that this is where we want to live and that we want to be a part of helping build a stronger town."

"I hope you're right. I guess I'm on the outside a little."

Patrick started to invite Chase to church but he wasn't going to push. "You might as well join us working on Opal Parker's house a few blocks over. We're going to patch up the roof in a week or so."

"I might do that. Thanks, Patrick." Chase pointed toward the This 'N' That. "Here comes Ann Mars, a woman with a mission."

"She stays busier than any woman I know."

"I don't know, Gracie Wilson seems to have her beat." Chase gave him a quick look and a smile. "She's something else."

"Ann?"

"Gracie."

Fortunately Ann had reached them and Patrick didn't have to answer the question Chase hadn't really asked.

"You boys look like trouble." Ann looked up at them. "And I get a catch in my neck looking up at you."

Patrick smiled at the older woman in her floral dress and orthopedic shoes. "Ann, you know we don't cause trouble."

She cackled at that. "Of course you don't. Why don't you walk with me, Patrick? I haven't checked in on you lately and I also haven't seen the displays the schoolkids set up."

He offered her his arm. "I'd love to walk with you."

Coffee could wait. He and Ann walked down the sidewalk and crossed Bronson Avenue. The school fund-raisers were set up on tables just down from the Cozy Cup Café. Maybe he'd get that coffee after all.

"There's Coraline." Ann tightened her grip on his arm and he could tell she was getting tired. "She retired but it didn't slow her down at all."

"She does stay busy." He spotted Coraline. She was talking to a few ladies who were standing behind the tables.

He and Ann slowed to look at a display of candles. The woman behind the table explained how much money would go to the school. Patrick didn't really need candles, but it was for a good cause.

"You can always give the candles to Gracie," Ann Mars offered as she ordered two candles for herself. "A girl always likes a nice candle. I think Gracie would like the cinnamon-apple scent."

"Thanks, Ann." He shook his head as he placed the order, pulling money from his pocket to pay. "I think."

"You should thank me. I know what I'm doing."

He was sure she did. But the question remained, what was *he* doing? A few months ago Ann Mars and Coraline Connolly had brought him the perfect employee. Gracie Wilson knew her way around the hardware store. She had the ability to build a cabinet or sand a table. She could install a light fixture or fix a plumbing problem. She charmed his customers with her easy smile and ability to laugh.

Now he had to figure out how she'd become more than just the perfect employee and what exactly he planned to do about it. He guessed the first step would be finding out what she felt about him.

Chapter Sixteen

The house Gracie had grown up in smelled of roast beef, potatoes and warm bread. The lovely aroma was a cover-up for the big mess her dad and brothers had made of the house since she moved out. She'd never seen it like this, with dust on the tables, dirty socks scattered around the living room and tea glasses left on coffee tables. She looked around the living room, disgusted by the mess. Who lived like this?

Oh, she knew—her dad and the brothers who still lived at home. Namely Evan. She blamed herself. She should have made him pick up after himself. She should have taught him to cook. Instead she'd picked up after him, washed his clothes and told him what to wear when he went on dates.

Being free from taking care of men had been a dream come true. But she missed it. She missed the rowdy meals, the last-minute farm chores. She missed home.

Not enough to move back, though. Being on her own meant discovering who she was without one of the Wilson men always looking over her shoulder and supervising her choices.

"What are you doing in here?" Her brother Jason walked through the front door. He stomped his feet to clean mud off his shoes and then jerked off the boots he'd worn out to the barn.

"Take your shoes off outside."

"Since when do you tell us to take off our shoes?" He opened the front door and stepped onto the porch. From outside he yelled, "Seriously, isn't that what the broom is for?"

She knew he was teasing but it made her mad anyway. "I no longer clean up after you guys."

"Right, and you miss it." He stepped back inside, his feet bare.

"You need a wife."

"You should have been married by now." He opened his mouth and she knew he was about to apologize for the joke. "Sis…"

"No, do not say you're sorry for joking. I'm ready to get back to joking and laughing. I don't want everyone worrying that they'll say the wrong thing. It's been almost a month."

"That isn't very long, Grace."

"I know." She picked up a couple of dirty glasses. "But I really am okay."

Jason picked up some dirty dishes. "Sorry about the mess. So, Dad said Patrick Fogerty is going to be here for lunch."

"Yes, and try not to say anything stupid."

"I'm not going to say anything to him. But I kind of wondered if the two of you were dating."

"Of course we aren't."

"Gotcha. Wishing?"

She pushed past him without answering and headed for the kitchen. "See if you can dust off the dining-room table so we can eat there."

"Will do."

"Do you know where Dad is? He left church when I did." Gracie peeked back in the dining room. Jason had grabbed a towel off the back of a chair and was wiping the table.

"What are you doing?"

"Dusting?" He held the towel up for her to see.

"That's a bath towel." She shuddered. "Single men are pigs."

"Most of the time. But if we don't have a woman here to tell us we're pigs, what does it matter? Remember, if a tree falls in the woods…"

Gracie looked heavenward and headed back to the kitchen. "I give up."

"Hey, does Patrick know you can't cook?" Jason shouted from the dining room.

The front door banged shut.

"He'll figure that out." A voice called out from the living room. Patrick's voice.

Jason walked into the kitchen carrying the dirty towel and a few more dirty dishes. He grinned and she grabbed the sprayer hose on the sink and silently threatened to turn on the water. He backed away still grinning.

Patrick walked through the doorway from the dining room with her younger brother, Evan. Gracie let go of the sprayer and smiled, but her insides were Jell-O, so her bravery was just pretend. Evan and Jason left. Patrick stood in the center of the big, country kitchen with the harvest-gold appliances and white linoleum floors.

Gracie looked around, unsure of what to do or say. She'd never had so many unsure moments in her life as she'd had in the past month.

"Would you like tea?" She reached into the cabinet for a glass.

Patrick grinned and she needed more than a glass of tea to distract her.

"That would be great." He walked to the sink

and turned on the water. As she fixed his glass of tea, he washed his hands. "Your dad is here."

"Is he?" She pulled the tea pitcher out of the fridge. "I don't know where he went after church."

Patrick continued to watch out the window. Gracie studied him from behind, the plaid shirt over broad shoulders, the dark hair cut short. Her boss. She needed to remember that, to not make things more complicated. For a long time she'd tried to tell herself he was kind and decent, he was attractive, and that was all there was to their relationship.

Now she knew better. She knew that she had fallen in love with him. Where did that leave her? She sighed and he moved, drawing her attention back to his face.

"He has someone with him." He took the glass of tea and the pitcher from her hands. He placed the pitcher on the counter and wrapped an arm around her shoulder.

"Someone?"

"A woman." He leaned down to whisper.

Her dad had brought a woman to Sunday lunch? This was how people moved on. Her dad had been alone for almost fifteen years. For the first time in all of those years, he was bringing a woman home to meet his family.

Gracie knew that it was time. So why did it hurt to think about her dad with someone else?

"Okay, a woman." She took a deep breath. "It's about time."

"Are you okay?"

She smiled up at him. "Yes, I'm good."

She wanted to tell him she was ready to move on. Maybe it hadn't taken her months or years, but her heart hadn't been shattered by loss. Her dad's heart had been broken to the point that it had taken years to mend.

Her heart had been misused. And now her heart was reaching out, wanting to find real love. Too soon?

"The roast smells good," he offered with another smile, this one teasing.

"You're wondering if it's edible."

"Maybe a little."

The front door banged and a few minutes later her dad was in the kitchen holding the hand of the lovely widow Wilma Duggins. Wilma smiled a shy smile.

"Gracie, I hope you don't mind that Jake invited me to have lunch with you all." Wilma smiled at Gracie's dad, and Gracie couldn't remember the last time someone called him Jake. To everyone in town he was Jacob Wilson.

"Of course I don't mind."

Gracie managed a smile. She had meant it. She didn't mind. But it would take a little more to come to terms with the changes taking place in her life, even in her heart.

Patrick watched Gracie as her dad and his new friend left the kitchen. Gracie's brother Jason escaped and headed out the back door. From the window Patrick saw him join two of the other brothers, who were walking up from the barn. Jacob Wilson dating seemed to be a pretty big deal.

"Can I help set the table?" Patrick offered, walking up behind Gracie as she pulled the roast from the oven.

"Do you mind?" She set the roast on the counter and reached to open the cabinet. He tried, because he was a gentleman, to ignore the way her pretty red dress slid up her legs when she reached.

He cleared his throat and she dropped to her heels again and looked at him.

"I can get those," he offered, because the plates were out of her reach.

"I'm sure you can. So can I. When I lived at home, I kept them on the counter." She had her hands on the counter behind her and she hopped up, landing with ease.

From her seat on the counter, she reached the plates and handed them to him. The two of them were nearly eye level. She smiled at him and pink climbed from her neck to her cheeks.

"Very resourceful," he whispered as he stepped close.

"I'm used to doing what I have to, Patrick. I've been climbing up to these cabinets most of my life."

"Did you ever think of getting a step stool?" He smiled as he said it and she laughed.

At the back of his mind, he knew to pull back, to keep this from going too far. Instead he gave in. He set the stack of plates on the counter and moved in front of her. He brushed a hand through her hair and as he did she leaned forward, her hands settling on his shoulders.

"I really should know better," he whispered just before his lips touched hers. He didn't know better, obviously. He knew that no other woman had ever made him forget his good sense. No other woman had ever made him want to think about white picket fences and a minivan full of kids.

The back door opened. He pulled away, and when he did she wiped her finger across his lips. She smiled a sweet smile.

"You don't look good in that shade of red," she whispered.

"I'll try to remember that."

Her brother Jason stomped back into the house. "Hey, are we going to eat today?"

Jason stopped and stared at them, shook his head and walked out of the room. Evan, Daniel and Caleb came in next. The Wilson brothers were all dark haired, tall and built like men who had worked hard all their lives. Patrick wouldn't want to tangle with any of them. Which was why he stepped away from Gracie and let her hop to the ground. He still held her hand and she gave his fingers a last squeeze before letting go.

"Time to eat." She smiled up at him as she grabbed a serving platter out of a lower cabinet.

Thirty minutes later Patrick sat back at the dining-room table surrounded by Wilsons who were obviously curious about his relationship with their sister. Fortunately they left him alone and instead asked Wilma Duggins twenty questions about her son in Afghanistan.

"The roast was dry," Gracie said, leaning in to whisper.

He didn't want to agree, but Evan heard and answered.

"Dry? Sis, the Sahara is dry. Arizona is dry. That roast was beyond dry."

"Thanks, Evan." She wadded up a napkin and threw it at him.

"So, Patrick." Caleb Wilson addressed him, grinning. "You're the rebound man?"

"Caleb, enough." Jacob cleared his throat. "Remember that we have guests. And let's give Gracie a break. She offered to cook us lunch and we're not going to complain."

"Does that mean we can question *you?*" Jason laughed as he aimed the question at his dad.

"You can clear the table and do the dishes." Jacob stood. "Wilma and I are going to town."

Patrick watched as the family dispersed. He'd grown up in a much smaller family with parents who rarely communicated. Sunday dinners together had been a rare thing. The Wilsons, all grown but still close to one another and to their father, stood and started clearing the table.

Gracie moved next to him. Suddenly she was out of her seat and he had to hurry to catch up. He followed her outside, catching up with her as she went down the front steps.

"Gracie."

She shook her head and kept walking. Patrick reached for her arm and she stopped. She didn't turn to face him. He walked up behind her, stopping with his hands on her arms.

"I'm sorry." She shivered in the cool air of late

September. Patrick ran his hands up her arms and pulled her back against him. "It's too much."

"What's too much?"

"My dad moving on. You."

"Me?"

"I'm not sure what to do, Patrick. A month ago I was getting married." She turned to face him. "I don't know what I feel. What if you are...?"

"The rebound?" He didn't know what else to say.

"I don't know. I look at my dad finally moving on after fifteen years. And my heart is already trying to move on."

"I think your story and your dad's are completely different."

"Maybe."

He lifted her chin with his finger and leaned down to kiss her lightly. "I understand. You need time, Gracie. Time to live on your own. Time to figure out what you want and who you want."

Maybe they both needed to step back and take time.

He'd never been the man who rushed into things, and the fact that he wanted to rush straight into a relationship with the woman he'd found just a month ago crying, still in her wedding dress, was maybe something he should think about.

"You should go home." She touched his cheek.

"Maybe I should." He kissed her and then walked away, looking back once to see her still standing where he'd left her.

When he drove into town a few minutes later, he stopped at The Everything to put gas in his truck and to buy a gallon of milk. Velma was at the register. She looked up from her book when he walked through the door.

"Hey, didn't you have lunch at the Wilson place today?" Velma dog-eared the page of her book, closed it and shoved it under the counter. Obviously she found his life more interesting than the romance novel she'd been reading.

"Yes, I did."

"Why do you look so glum, then?"

"I didn't realize I looked glum." He walked back to the cooler, got his milk and headed back to the register. Velma was situated on her stool, waiting.

"Maybe not glum. Maybe confused. It's like that when you fall in love. And a man your age should know that. Have you been living under a rock?"

Laughter took him by surprised. "No, but I haven't spent a lot of time on relationships."

"This took you by surprise, then?"

Okay, the ball was obviously in her court. "I guess it did. But I think it also took Gracie by surprise."

"She'll work through it. Life takes us by surprise sometimes. We make a plan and suddenly the plan isn't, and then we make a new plan. Gracie thought she'd be married and living in Manhattan by now. She wanted a place of her own."

"I'm sure she did."

"You're taken by surprise because you thought you'd try out a new life in a new town. You had a nice little employee who was getting married, and then she wasn't, and then you started falling in love with her."

He paid for the gas and the gallon of milk. "You read too many romance novels, Velma."

She laughed and leaned forward. "Yes, I do. But I can also spot a couple in love when I see one. Or at least falling in love. It's because I've lived awhile. I know the signs."

"What signs are those?" He leaned on the counter, unfortunately hooked on the crazy conversation with Velma in her tie-dyed T-shirt.

"Oh, the signs. A couple in love starts out with little looks. They start to share things. And then they start putting the other person first, taking care of each other, looking out for each other. Now, the common mistake is when a person thinks it's all about chemistry. Everyone loves the 'zing' of chemistry, but that zing isn't going to get you through fifty years of marriage."

"So you think I'm in love with Gracie?" He grinned and took the piece of dark chocolate Velma offered.

"I think you and Gracie have to figure that out for yourselves."

"Weren't you just saying…?"

She laughed and popped the dark chocolate into her mouth. "I said I know love when I see it. What's going on between you and Gracie is between you and Gracie."

"Velma, you trapped me again."

"I get bored sitting in here on a Sunday afternoon. Trapping you breaks up the monotony."

"I'll have to make sure I stop in more often and skip Sunday afternoons."

"You'll be back."

He probably would. But next time maybe he'd realize he was walking into one of Velma's traps. He laughed as he got into the truck. At least she'd helped clarify things for him. Now he just had to figure out what to do about it.

Chapter Seventeen

Gracie called in sick on Monday. Patrick didn't know if she was sick or avoiding him. He thought maybe it was best if they did have a little time apart, time to think. It created a problem when he needed his right-hand woman and she was the one he needed space from.

Especially since the block party had been a success. By Tuesday morning he couldn't run the store by himself, not even with Jeff coming in after school. When Coraline Connolly stopped by Tuesday midmorning, he knew what he had to do.

"Coraline, you're hired."

"I'm what?"

"You're hired. Here's your apron." He tossed the apron he pulled out from under the counter. She caught it but was still staring at him as if he'd fallen off the proverbial turnip truck.

"Where's Gracie?" Coraline, always game, slipped the apron over her head. It fit her better than it did Gracie.

"She's taking some time off." He rang up the sale for the gentleman standing at the register. He bagged the paint and lightbulbs, thanked the customer and straightened the work area.

"How much time off, Patrick?"

"I'm not really sure." He watched the customer walk out the door.

"I see." And she let it go.

Instead of discussing it, she went to work. By lunchtime she was an old pro at working the counter, and he found that she had a decent knowledge of nearly every type of home-remodeling project. She wasn't Gracie, but she was a good hand.

"Coraline, do you think this is enough?" He sat down next to her when there was a lull. They had a fresh cup of coffee and a few minutes to catch their breath.

"This? The help I'm giving you?" She smiled and sipped her coffee.

"The stores. I know that these stores bring business to town, but is it really enough to keep the school open or to keep the police and fire departments going? With homes being foreclosed and people moving, I know the property tax revenue is down. I love this town and Main Street, but I don't know if it'll save Bygones."

She sighed and took another sip of coffee before answering, "I don't know, Patrick. I really don't. What will you do if you can't keep this store going?"

"I don't want to leave."

"No, and we don't want you to go. I guess only time will tell. But you have more pressing matters. What are you going to do about Gracie Wilson?"

"I'm going to give her space."

"Wise man. She needs a little space and maybe a little time to figure out who she is on her own. Don't worry, she isn't going to walk away from this store."

He wanted to tell Coraline that he wasn't as worried about Gracie walking away from The Fixer-Upper as he was about her walking away from him. There were a lot of things he wanted to say that he didn't.

He had to fight the urge to close shop and drive over to Gracie's. As much as he wanted her to pick him, to pick them, he wouldn't push. She'd felt as if she had to go through with the marriage to Trent, even after she caught him cheating. He never wanted there to be a question about the two of them.

If he had to give her time to realize what they had, he'd give her time. But not too much.

After three days of sitting in her little house, alternately praying and staring at walls, Gracie had finally come to some very strong conclusions. And those conclusions required action.

She tossed aside the blanket she'd been wrapped up in, carried her coffee cup to the kitchen and started step one of her plan. She opened her closet and started throwing clothes onto the bed. She picked up a pretty dress, black and shimmery. She thought she'd worn it to a formal dinner in college. She held it up, wrinkled her nose and tossed it back to the bed with the other rejects.

Jeans and a nice top. She shook her head. A nice dress she often wore to church? No. Not that it wasn't a pretty dress, but it didn't quite have the appeal she wanted. Finally she settled on the red dress she'd worn to church Sunday. She smiled as she lifted it off the pile of clean clothes she had yet to hang and put away.

Perfect.

Next, hair and makeup. She almost never wore makeup, but she did own some and she did know how to apply it when necessary. And she owned a flat iron for her hair. Not that she ever used it. Tonight required all of the weapons in her female arsenal.

She had spent months trying to find Patrick Fogerty the right woman, and the right woman had been under his nose the entire time. She was the right woman for Patrick. She hadn't realized it for a while. Or maybe she had but she'd tried to deny it.

How could she love Patrick after such a short time and after an almost wedding? It had occurred to her that she'd grown to love him slowly over time. In the past week or so she'd recognized that he was the person who made her feel whole. He completed her life as no one ever had.

She had to show him and convince him to give her a chance.

She had almost made a mess of her life. God had redeemed the mess because He'd had another plan the whole time. God had opened a door for Patrick to come to Bygones.

It took her an hour to get ready and she walked out of the house. She looked around, hoping no one would see her climbing into her truck to go after her man. But he was hers and she was determined to make that known.

When she pulled up to the back of the store, his truck wasn't there. She parked and got out.

He'd be back soon. Maybe he'd gone to church. Or maybe…

She sat down on the steps that led to his apartment. Maybe he'd gone out with one of the women she'd fixed him up with. Her heart sank a little as she sat there waiting. Inside his apartment she heard Rufus bark at the door. Even the dog was tired of waiting.

Or maybe wondering when he'd come home.

She had no one to blame but herself. She'd let him leave her dad's without telling him how she felt. She'd asked him for time off from work. He'd had to bring Coraline in to help him.

Headlights flashed. Patrick's truck pulled up behind hers. For a long minute he sat behind the wheel and then he got out and walked past her truck to the steps. She stood as he was pulling keys out of his pocket.

"So this is where you've been." He walked past her, up the steps to the door. "I've been at your place. I was worried about you."

"I've been sitting here thinking you might be on a date. I did fix you up with some really nice women."

He reached inside the door for a leash and snapped it on the dog's collar. The big, scruffy animal jumped and lurched from the apartment.

"I need to walk him. You can wait here or walk with us."

Gracie followed him down the stairs. Rufus kept the leash pulled tight in his excitement. Gracie hurried to keep up with the dog's excitement and Patrick's longer stride.

"He's glad to be outside." Gracie caught up.

"I'm glad you finally came out of your house. I was so worried about you. I tried your house, Velma's and Coraline's. I even knocked on Ann's door."

"I'm sorry. I just needed time."

"I know."

She took the hand he offered. "You always understand. Do you understand how exasperating I can be to the average person?"

He laughed at that. The dog sniffed at bushes and lunged at a rabbit, which escaped. They kept walking.

"I know you need space to figure out what you want."

"You."

He pulled Rufus to a stop and turned to face her. The wind blew her hair. He brushed it back and then he leaned down and kissed her gently.

"I need you, too."

Gracie's heart sang as she touched his cheek and he kissed her again. The dog moved around them, sniffing the ground and wrapping them close in his leash. Patrick laughed and nuzzled her hair, then her ear. His arms went around her.

"Hold still. Rufus is tying us together."

"Smart dog." Gracie held still as Patrick moved, pulling the dog to unwrap them from the leash.

"Very smart." Patrick kissed her again. "He's missed you, too."

They were untangled and the dog pulled in the other direction. Patrick held the leash in one hand and wrapped the other arm around Gracie. She needed him in her life.

"You're not the rebound man."

"Okay."

"You're the only man I want in my life." The words were out and she waited, wanting to be the only woman he needed in his life. Her heart ached as she waited.

Patrick held the leash, watching as Rufus sniffed around a tree and then tugged, trying to go in another direction. The animal was too big to be kept inside. He needed a fenced yard. Gracie moved and he looked down at her sweet, upturned face.

The woman he hadn't known he needed. He looked up, laughing a little at how God worked.

"I've never known what it would feel like. I questioned if I would know."

She shook her head. "What?"

"I'm the product of a broken home. I took myself to church. I grew my own faith. I knew that someday, if I got married, it would be forever. I didn't know if I would know how it felt to meet a woman I wanted in my life forever. What if I didn't know?"

"I can tell you what it doesn't feel like." She half smiled but he saw the remnants of the pain left behind from her failed attempt at a wedding.

"I can tell you what it feels like to know the person you're holding is someone you want to hold forever." He kissed her again. She felt sweet in his arms. She belonged there, with him. "It feels like this."

She sighed and touched his cheek. "What if there are times it doesn't?"

"Doesn't?"

"Feel like this?"

"Then we stick it out until it feels this way again. I'm not going to any more singles' meetings, Gracie. I'm only asking that you give us a chance."

"Yes." She reached for the leash he nearly dropped as he held her close. "I think this is definitely something to take a chance on."

"I'm glad, because I'm okay being your rebound man if it means being the only man in your life."

She kissed him again and then whispered next to his ear, "I love you."

He picked her up and hugged her. "I love you, too."

His lips touched hers as he set her back on her feet, on firm ground that wasn't so firm at the moment. He loved her. And this time it was real; she knew the difference in her heart. The next time Gracie Wilson made plans to walk down the aisle of a church, he would be the man waiting for her. She closed her eyes and dreamed of a wedding that she would plan, and it ended with her in the arms of Patrick Fogerty.

Gracie Fogerty. She smiled as they linked arms and finished their walk.

* * * * *

LARGER-PRINT BOOKS!

GET 2 FREE
LARGER-PRINT NOVELS
PLUS 2 FREE
MYSTERY GIFTS

Love Inspired®

Larger-print novels are now available...

LILPDIR13R

ReaderService.com

Manage your account online!

- Review your order history
- Manage your payments
- Update your address

---

*We've designed
the Harlequin® Reader Service
website just for you.*

Enjoy all the features!

- Reader excerpts from any series
- Respond to mailings and
  special monthly offers
- Discover new series available to you
- Browse the Bonus Bucks catalog
- Share your feedback

Visit us at:

ReaderService.com